THE VENOMOUS PEACE

THE VENOMOUS PEACE

PRASHANTH CHAKKULA

simplicitè
Books ◈ Blog ◈ Literary Services

Live Simple. Live Simplicité.
Email: livesimplicite@gmail.com

The Venomous Peace.

A Simplicité Initiative – 2025.
ISBN: 978-93-5898-374-6

Edited by: Kopal Mittal (Risa Rey Literary Services)
Typeset at Minion Pro, Garamond & Times New Roman
By Shubham Singh, Team Simplicité
Cover Design by: Team Simplicité

Co-Published by

Qurate Books Pvt. Ltd.
Goa 403523, India
www.quratebooks.com
Tel: 1800-210-6527, Email: info@quratebooks.com

THE CHARACTERS

Carrying insurmountable pain in his eyes, Rishi languidly strolled in a busy street and headed towards a housing area. It was noon when he took shelter under the shade of a tree. People around him didn't seem to trouble him, but his eyes were glued to one point. Heavy thoughts tend to make people pause and reflect, and stability is directly proportional to the pain a person carries within. The state of Rishi seemed as if he was going to make a life-altering decision, but his body language stood him unsure of his actions. He sat unmoved as the sun set gradually, and people got off their daily duties and shopped around the street. The time passed to such a state where finding people in the street seemed impossible.

The environment slowly triggered the still Rishi to head towards a known house in the locality. He waited outside the house for a few minutes before knocking on the door. A known face answered the door and was surprised to see Rishi. The known man inquired about the same, but Rishi didn't respond. He then asked Rishi to enter. As the man turned back into the house, Rishi slit the back of his neck with a sharp object. The cut is so deep that the man started growing unconscious. However, he forced himself to turn back to comprehend what Rishi was trying to do. As the man faced Rishi, he now slit the front of his neck with the same object. With enough blood spattering around for a person to lose their pulse, the man completely lost his consciousness. Rishi quickly left the house and disappeared into the pitch dark. He didn't seem troubled by the act that he had just performed.

If hurting a person doesn't hurt you, what is it called? Hate? Anger?

Months passed by. One fine day, Rishi, who had hidden in a village, answered the knocking on the door and was surprised to see police walking in with a warrant to arrest him. He confessed to his crime when the police showed him enough evidence. He was taken into custody and had been on trial for several months, and one fine day, he received a verdict to serve life imprisonment. Twenty-five years passed by.

❖

Avni and Adi, mental health counselors at the same clinic, saw patients together for therapy and counseling sessions in one of the treatment rooms. After a distressing session with a struggling patient, Avni remained quiet even after the session ended.

Avni was still processing what had transpired during their difficult conversation. The patient was crying at several intense moments, expressing hopelessness. The case deeply impacted and moved Avni.

Adi noticed Avni's silence and glanced at her curiously, wondering if she was okay. Avni eventually spoke, commenting on how hard it was to hear the patient describe such suffering and isolation. Adi nodded in agreement, reflecting on the session and how they might help the patient going forward.

Avni expressed her concern, "How can we help a patient who feels hurt and offended by loved ones when, as counselors, we ourselves may not have all the answers?"

Dr. Adi responded, "Ultimately, the most important question is–what do you perceive as insulting or hurtful?"

Avni replied thoughtfully, understanding Adi, who aimed to shift her focus from judging others' actions to understanding the patient's emotions and perspective. "Perhaps these conversations wouldn't feel so hurtful if they weren't coming from loved ones."

Adi probed further, interested in understanding Avni's perspective more deeply. "Why do you think conversations with loved ones cause more pain than others?"

Avni reflected, "Criticism from loved ones carries more weight. They're the ones I value the most. It feels like a judgment on my character when it comes from them."

Adi nodded. "That makes sense. Our close relationships come with higher expectations." The doctor then shifted the focus towards solutions. "Still, we have a choice in how we allow others' words to affect us. For the sake of discussion, imagine if I were to say, 'I hate your green eyes.' How do you think you might react?" Adi posed a hypothetical scenario.

"I'd likely just laugh it off," Avni responded promptly.

The doctor probed further, "And why do you think laughing it off might be your instinctive response?"

"I'm confident my eyes aren't green, so a comment about disliking 'green eyes' wouldn't affect me."

"So, you wouldn't feel bad if I say that I hate the quality of you having green eyes?"

"It wouldn't really bother me as that was not me," Avni responded.

The doctor acknowledged Avni's perspective while gently encouraging her to consider alternative responses. "So, when you can physically distinguish that the qualities people perceive don't apply to you, you accept their comments wholeheartedly. But why don't you have the same peace of mind when people criticize you with rather emotionally indistinguishable qualities?"

"Like what?" Avni was puzzled.

"If someone you love calls you a cruel, wicked, and

inhumane person?"

Avni remained silent, realizing the importance of the conversation.

The doctor continued, "People are mysterious. The characteristics we fail to observe in others often cause us the most pain because we can never know what's in their head. For instance, if I tell you – I have color blindness and say I don't like your green eyes, how might you interpret my words?"

"At first, I might be hurt. But I can understand that your comment has nothing to do with my eyes, and instead, it is completely your perception of my eyes. I would explain this to you, respecting your perspective."

The doctor nodded. "Exactly, with clarity in thoughts and good communication, issues that initially cause hurt can often be solved. The important thing is focusing our energy on what we can control, rather than on what we cannot, for example, about what others would think."

"I would also like to know how you consider others' perspectives. Is it you stepping into others' shoes or considering yourself as the other person?"

"Wasn't it stepping into others' shoes?"

"No, then you may not be understanding the person. You are only trying to weigh the outcomes of your actions if you were the other person."

"Like how?" Avni was curious.

"Suppose I felt that you made an error, which could be unintentional, and I question your work. Even after putting in your best efforts, how would you reflect on the situation?" Adi waited for Avni's response.

"I would appreciate you pointing out that I acted unintentionally. I will be careful to avoid making the same mistake again." Avni sounded sensible.

"I can understand that you acted unintentionally when I

approach the situation from your perspective, using the skills and knowledge that you possess. Not just from my own perspective."

Avni looked puzzled. "Let me elaborate a bit," Adi answered the unspoken question.

"When I think I am Avni, I feel like I did my best, based on my training and experience. If the outcome was not ideal, then I would feel like I need to improve my skills, and then I believe it was an honest mistake, and I would accept it peacefully. However, if I tried to put myself 'in your shoes', I might judge harshly as I judged the situation through my skill lens and your ability to perform. I would think, 'How could you make such a silly mistake?' This would lead to insults, regrets, pain, and anger. So, you must be careful in taking others' perspectives."

Avni agreed, "You're right. Dwelling on what someone else may or may not be thinking only takes me away from my peace of mind." She thought about her situation with Chetan and his family.

"Wonderfully put. It seems we're on the same page here. The cause of hurt lies not in others' words, but in how we interpret and react to them. This realization alone can lessen our suffering."

Avni listened carefully to the doctor's answer, taking his advice. She realized that it was essential to understand each patient's unique perspective and experiences in order to provide the best possible care. Although Avni is convinced, she remains thoughtful.

"Is there anything that I can further help with?" Adi asked her.

Avni replied tensely, "It's been long since I last spoke with Chetan. His family needs time to consider our marriage proposal. As days pass, I am not ready to have any difficult conversations. This has been making me anxious lately."

"I can't help but wonder what reservations they may have

about me. Perhaps cultural differences, personality incompatibilities, or other complex factors. Without open communication, it's hard to figure out. I have started to think that this might impact my future relations with his family. I need to stop overthinking and focus on building our relationship."

"It sounds like an uncomfortable situation, made more difficult by a lack of communication. Please consider initiating a direct conversation with Chetan. Being transparent about your feelings could help move things forward, for better or worse." Adi consoled.

"You're right."

"Don't worry, there is always hope. Darkness never lasts forever, and light eventually breaks through, guiding our next steps to write better than what was written yesterday," assured Adi.

"Thank you, doctor!" She was feeling grateful for the conversation. "I think I just need to focus on myself."

The doctor smiled warmly and asked her to brief him about the next patient. "Before we move on to the next patient, I want to remind you that the parole board members have requested your time again for Rishi."

Adi sighed, wondering why they were so focused on him. "Since when did parole board members seem so invested in an inmate's release?" Adi signaled Avni to respond to the prison that he will attend.

❖

Chetan's mind was one to wander off into the abyss of mysteries. He was a private detective, unraveling clues and secrets had become his addiction. The job had taken him to dark places, which most people never see. Witnessing greed, betrayal, and violence had become a routine. Some cases kept him awake at night, wrestling with the remains of people's shattered lives.

He was on his way to visit his mother, who lived nearby. Although her business kept her mostly busy, she always managed to make time for Chetan and his brother. Indira, Chetan's mother, followed certain principles in raising and supporting her children when they needed her.

She followed her belief that until her child turned 18, she would spend 90% of her controllable time with them; after that, she felt it was up to them to take charge of their own lives. Upon growing up, Chetan had become a criminologist, and his brother– a businessman. They lived independently yet close by. Indira taught them to be kind and helpful to a great extent. She ingrained deep values in them about making positive impacts, beyond personal successes.

However, chasing criminals, murderers, and revealing the reasons for murders had adversely affected Chetan's mindset. He felt excluded from society. He is against the nonsensical perspective that usually influenced people. He had seen so much that he didn't want to believe the truth where people show their true colours. It's sad to see when grown-ups become scared of the light that reveals the truth.

After working on many mystery and murder cases, the saturation of Chetan's mind was breaking day by day. Though Indira saw his talents and success, she did not know the darkness his work had brought him. He remained silent until now as he did not want to show weakness before discussing his marriage with Avni. Silence was too much for him now, but he hesitated to be weak. Lately, the cases he has been dealing with have made a mess in his mind. His only hope was talking to his mother, who could help him.

He was a successful detective in his thirties, who eventually became depressed and alienated in a problematic situation. Nothing was more frustrating than seeing Chetan doing fantastic work–solving cases and providing justice–but coming home exhausted, irritable, and hostile.

Chetan saw his brother Vinay waiting for him. He was surprised. "Vinay! What are you doing here?"

Vinay responded casually, "Didn't Mom call and ask you to come?"

Chetan was curious, "No, I am surprised to see you. Is everything okay?"

"There isn't a big problem, but Mom seems a little upset about something with the business." Vinay sounded concerned. Chetan's brow furrowed.

"Upset, how?"

"I'm not really sure... but it didn't seem serious."

"Shall we speak to her?"

"I just spoke to her, it is your turn now," his brother asked Chetan to go alone, and he gestured towards their mother's room. "I will go speak to her," said Chetan.

Chetan shared a close bond with his kind, loving mother, who taught him about love, kindness, and compassion. She was overjoyed to see her son and welcomed him with open arms.

"How come you're here?" She asked about his sudden visit.

"You seem tired?" Said his mother, holding him tightly.

"How have you been?" Chetan asked his mother.

"I am good, but I don't see the same in you. Is it related to Avni?" She questioned Chetan, still holding him in her arms.

"I hope you understand that I must have a good reason if I hesitate to share something with you," Indira said in response to Chetan's unspoken question about the decision for his upcoming wedding with Avni.

Indira continued, "I want you to know that if I withhold anything from you, it is for your own good. Being your mother, I need to take measures to protect you. I will always act with your best interests in mind."

She touched his arm and continued, "You must trust that I

would never keep something from you without cause."

"No, it is not about Avni. Vinay told me that you were upset with some business?" Chetan showed interest in his mother's agony, redirecting the topic to avoid embarrassment.

"I know when to burden you with the business. I can handle it."

"If it is not Avni, it must be related to your work. Are you stressed?"

Chetan remained silent. He wanted to discuss himself, but hesitated to interrupt the moment.

THE OBLIGATION

Lalit, an experienced Chartered Accountant, expected a busy day assisting high-profile clients with business recovery, insolvency, and taxation by analyzing their financial records.

Arriving early, he greeted staff with a smile, addressing any issues immediately. He started the day by taking a moment to mentally prepare, reviewing his to-do list, and prioritizing the most urgent tasks.

Lalit analyzed the financial statements of a manufacturing company struggling with liquidity issues. The procedure flowed from recognizing potential cost cuts and revenue gains to drafting a recovery plan for the management to implement immediately.

He reviewed a client's key facts and figures, considering various arguments to build a strong case. He called the client, provided the requested information, and prepared for any follow-up questions. He then outlined a tailored strategy based on his analysis, experience, and understanding of the client's needs.

Lalit met his clients outside the office each afternoon. Upon realizing that many of them were too busy to visit, he bought lunch from a roadside stall. While waiting in line, a stranger tried to converse with him. Lalit politely responded, but the stranger seemed to lose interest. Lalit, used to the peculiarities of city life, remained focused on his day.

After a quick meal, he headed back to the office. He spent

the afternoon finalizing accounts, assessing clients' systems to identify solutions, analyzing risks, and ensuring sound financial controls. He then met a steady stream of clients–small business owners to corporate executives–approaching each unique case with diligence, patience, and recommendations tailored to their needs.

As the sun set and the office gradually emptied, mentally drained but satisfied, Lalit gathered his notes. Another busy day was over, and he headed home mentally planning for the next day's challenges.

On his way home, Lalit stopped by the gym–a routine that helped him stay focused and productive throughout long days of analyzing complex client cases.

After the workout, Lalit again encountered the stranger from back in the day. "Are you following me?" He joked. "Not at all," the stranger chuckled, "simply a coincidence." He paused before speaking again. "Actually, I have a personal finance issue that requires an expert's help. I was told an accountant like you could provide some guidance." Though a stranger, his request for financial guidance seemed genuine to Lalit. "I'd be happy to listen and offer any advice I can."

The sky was overcast, and a cool breeze rustled the trees as both men walked past the gym parking lot. Streetlights flickered as night descended over the city's outskirts.

The stranger led Lalit to a secluded spot, quiet and empty. Before Lalit could question the unusual location, the man suddenly attacked, wrapping a cloth tightly around his neck from behind. Lalit struggled, but the assault was swift and overpowering. Gasping for air, he fought to break free, yet the stranger's grip was relentless, keeping him out of reach. As Lalit grew visibly weak and breathless, the attacker finally loosened his hold and pretended to walk away, leaving an eerie silence behind.

After a few minutes, Lalit slowly regained consciousness, but his body remained weak and unsteady. Even with some strength returning, he was unable to make his way to his vehicle. Suddenly, he heard a sharp sound of shattering glass, followed by approaching footsteps. A wave of fear washed over him as he realized he was not alone, and still too vulnerable to defend himself.

The stranger returned, this time with deadlier intent. Without hesitation, he slashed Lalit's throat with a sharp piece of glass, ensuring there was no chance of survival. He watched coldly as Lalit took his final breath, then vanished into the shadows, leaving the lifeless body in a pool of blood.

❖

Chetan received a call the next morning and immediately reached the spot. The murderer stuffed Lalit's lifeless body in Lalit's car trunk. There was little evidence to start with. Though known for his keen powers of deduction, Chetan was distracted by the current headspace and found it hard to focus on work.

His focus had not been great of late. He had started to think of himself as a failure, unable to return to his usual self. He reminisced about the days when investigating crimes filled him with excitement. Lately, the emotional response to such cases lingered, and he felt overwhelmed.

After carefully examining the body, Chetan noted the absence of surveillance at the crime scene. The limited evidence pointed to a complex investigation ahead. He studied the collected evidence in his office, determined to find anything that might crack the case.

When Chetan first began investigating crimes, he approached each case with excitement and curiosity, eager to uncover clues and solve the mystery. There was something enjoyable about piecing together evidence and following threads of information to arrive at the truth.

However, the experience brought him a sobering realization. Behind every crime lies darker human truth motives born from greed, hatred, and depravity. The more Chetan learned about the circumstances and context surrounding a crime, the more unpleasant the reality he must confront.

Chetan was so tired that he didn't want this anymore. Interestingly, he didn't know exactly what he didn't want anymore. Was it solving cases? Was it the job? Was it the responsibility? Or was it the relationship? Whenever he tried to focus on a case, the only thing that came out was rage and shame at letting someone down. To divert his anxiety, he visited his mother's place.

Two days in a row? That's a surprise? His mother welcomed him. His brother, who was already there, greeted him. Upon talking, his mother observed that Chetan was stressed.

Indira spoke with Chetan about how pleased she was with how he had fulfilled his duties with skill and sincerity.

"I would like you to continue being helpful in the same way. I am so proud of the happy childhood I could give you," she said.

Indira had always done her best to provide for her sons and ensure they had a positive upbringing.

Indira seemed to enjoy Chetan's company while chatting on the sofa. Suddenly, Indira tried to stand up but lost her balance and fell back onto the couch. Chetan quickly reached out to steady her with concern. Indira explained that physically she had become weak, but emotionally she remained strong due to her sons' successful work. Vinay then joined them, enquiring about dinner.

Sitting on the sofa, Indira asked Chetan to pass her the eye drops she used for her dry eyes. He handed them to her carefully, and as she applied them, he held her hand gently. It was a small gesture showing that he genuinely cared for her well-being.

Chetan was heartbroken to see his mother in such a state. He vowed to take care of her and keep his promise, no matter what. He didn't feel that he had control over emotions that could give room to discuss sensitive issues. He was tied to his responsibility of caring for his mother rather than troubling her with his challenges. When you love someone, there is no control, and that's what love is. The three of them then went to the dining hall for dinner.

Chetan's mother watched him closely as he picked at his dinner, moving the food around his plate without eating much. He had been quiet and withdrawn.

After dinner, Indira, Vinay, and Chetan sit in the lounge surfing various topics. Vinay led most of the discussion by initiating different subjects, with Indira and Chetan going along.

Indira noticed that Chetan did not seem as enthusiastic or proactive as usual. His responses lacked his usual energy and input. She wondered if everything was alright with Chetan. She sat beside him and asked gently, "Son, what troubles you? You seem sad." Indira spoke about the pain and discomfort she observed in his eyes.

Chetan hesitated but eventually surrendered and confessed about his work and how it was affecting him. Tears welled up as he said, "I'm such a disappointment." He discussed having a tough time dealing with the aftermath of a crime or murder.

His mother put her arm around him. "Listen to me," she said. "You don't have to apologize. We understand the complexity you are going through. I am here for you." She hugged him tightly.

"I am proud of your work, no matter how much I earn, I cannot gain the respect you have. You are kind, thoughtful, and full of potential. It's time that you become proud of yourself."

Chetan shook his head. "But I failed to process the trauma. I worked so hard and still failed."

Indira listened patiently and lifted his chin to look him in the eyes. "Will it be feasible for you to move here for a few days to stay with me until you feel okay?"

Chetan shook his head no.

"Life gives us many challenges. How we choose to respond is the true test of our character." She smiled at him. "I have faith in you, my son. Now have faith in yourself."

She reminded him that bringing justice and peace to the people was more potent than any stress or trauma he could face. "Don't hesitate to come out of pain to provide justice even if your family suffers."

Chetan threw his arms around his mother and closed his eyes. All the stress and worry came pouring out. His mother held him tightly, stroking his hair like when he was a child.

When the heaviness in the heart subsided, he looked at his mother and said, "Thank you. You always know how to make me feel better." She smiled.

"A mother's love has a magic all its own." Chetan smiled back. "I'm lucky to have you."

His mother hugged him close. "And I'm lucky to have you, my brave and brilliant boy."

"What about my luck?" Vinay interrupts. They all smile.

His mother continued, "Now, let's make a plan to conquer this challenge together, okay?" She told him to talk to Avni about his condition. Indira knew that Avni would be a great support system for him.

Chetan nodded. "Okay." Chetan wished to discuss his relationship with Avni openly, yet he hesitated to discuss such a sensitive subject. He was concerned about his mother's health, and he didn't want to stress her.

Chetan felt a sense of relief after spending time with his mother and brother, but the weight of his work and its darkness still seemed heavy on him. He knew he needed to find a way to cope with it and bring back the light in his life.

Despite being a renowned therapist, Chetan didn't want to burden Avni, his girlfriend, with his insecurities and weaknesses, as suggested by his mother before having a confirmed date for the wedding.

❖

"Good morning, doctor. It's great to see you again!" The prison psychologist greeted Adi, whom Avni accompanied. The psychologist, also a parole board member, enquired about Avni. "She's my colleague, and this is her first visit to the prison," Adi replied. "Don't worry, it won't be her last," joked the psychologist.

The three walked towards a cell where Rishi was serving his sentence. Avni asked the parole board member about their interest in Rishi, which prompted them to encourage him to apply for parole.

Adi remained silent, allowing his colleague to ask the question. The board member paused before explaining, "It also impacts the prison's reputation. Parole is typically granted by a parole board of appointed officials who review applications. Our members usually have backgrounds in criminal justice, law enforcement, psychology, or social work."

"Although parole eligibility depends on several factors, I can confidently say that in the past 25 years, Rishi has met all the criteria necessary for the board to approve his application." After his last session with Dr. Adi, Rishi had spent a couple of days outside under supervision to help acclimate to the external environment.

A member accompanied the doctors to Rishi's cell.

Rishi, who appeared older than his usual age, was lean and muscular, with eyes filled with warmth and kindness.

"How was your outing the other day?" The doctor asked, hoping for a positive response. Instead, Rishi broke down, pleading with the doctor not to suggest going outside again. He confessed that he had forgotten how to interact with normal people and feared how he would cope with the judgment from a crowd. He expressed his anxiety about feeling out of place in society.

Avni tried to interject, but Adi gently stopped her, focusing on comforting Rishi. After a moment, they both decided to leave the room.

"This stems from his fear of becoming normal again. We can't help him unless he opens up about what's keeping him confined and what makes him so afraid of the outside world."

"What shall we do now?"

"Wait for the right time as we do for the other patients," Adi responded to Avni.

Confused, Avni didn't get into the car. "Are you not coming with me?"

"I will meet Chetan and see you in the morning." Adi left, bidding goodbye to Avni.

THE WARMTH OF BEING TOGETHER

Chetan received a call from his girlfriend Avni, who was checking in on him. Though he had become less interested in socializing lately, he agreed to meet her. He was afraid of the conversation he would have, which would have more questions than answers. He did not want to give Avni false hopes about their marriage. He was also reluctant to talk about his traumatic experiences.

Chetan and Avni had moved on from falling in love to loving each other deeply. In the first phase, you only admire the positives of a person, whereas in the later phase, you admire the person with their flaws. However, Chetan found it challenging to show his weaknesses to his girlfriend.

As agreed, Avni waited for Chetan at the coffee shop. She arrived early, and he was late, as usual. Avni felt anxious and wished to have an honest discussion with Chetan about any potential concerns his parents might have about her. If Chetan's parents disagreed, what would her state be? The idea of losing Chetan caused Avni great anxiety. She could not stand the thought of ending their relationship.

Over these long years in the relationship, the couple had experienced all the extremes. Initially, they found joy in simple things like spending time together and learning about each other's lives. Over time, their conversations deepened as they understood each other more deeply.

Avni had known Chetan since their graduation days. They both pursued a bachelor's degree in psychology, after which she proceeded to the Central University to take the courses prescribed for psychiatrists. Chetan moved on to pursue a criminology degree for his master's. After his master's, he joined a private detective agency that hired criminologists.

Although she was with him throughout their graduation, she never knew what real love was. After a few days of their course completion, one of their simple meetings blossomed into something more. Avni's patience drew Chetan out of his shell, while Chetan's calm presence soothed Avni's restless spirit. Together, they realized love doesn't follow a plan–it finds you when you least expect it.

Though they were now working in different fields, their bond remained strong. However, work-life had taken the stage in defining the couple's behavior. A few months ago, Chetan's busy schedule often left little time for Avni, which made her feel lonely. Yet, Chetan's presence–whether a held hand, a voice over the phone, or even a smile–reassured Avni of his love. His absence made her miss him deeply, even if he was just in the next room.

Now, time had played a spoilsport for Avni. Though Avni had been excited to begin work with her mentor psychiatrist, the long hours and demands of the new job left little time for Chetan. Each day, she returned home exhausted, too tired to call the man who held her heart. Though they did not quarrel, a rift grew between them without intention. However, giving your heart to somebody is the scariest, most dangerous, and most distracting thing.

Although time means little when two souls are meant to be together, the rift growing between the couple was becoming dangerous day by day. Sometimes, they complained that one person had started investing more in their work routine than the other. The couple was slowly becoming distant.

It had been weeks since she had seen him. She couldn't find time to meet her boyfriend since she started working with a renowned psychiatrist, Adi. In the initial days, there used to be time to meet Chetan for a little while; however, it disappeared slowly. Adi left the office by five every evening; she stayed back till nine to draft all the notes she had taken from the patients on the table. She never had the foresight that managing time for Chetan would become challenging.

Avni felt a sense of unease, a hollowness that told her something was amiss. Though she saw Chetan in her thoughts, his absence now weighed heavily on her spirit. She wasn't wholly aware of his situation.

"Hello Avni, how are you doing? Has Chetan left you anticipating again?" greeted the waiter in the busy coffee shop. The sight of a friendly greeting in the great wilderness of her overthinking was pleasant. The waiter was a good-natured guy who worked there as a partner and had been a good companion to the couple. He appeared to be delighted. Lacking enthusiasm, she sighed and said, "As always." She ordered food to kill time and save herself from the embarrassment of sitting at an empty table in a busy coffee shop.

"Is everything alright? It's been quite a while since you came here," asked the waiter. "It's almost two months, and unfortunately Chetan and I have barely spent time with each other in these months." Based on her rapport with the waiter, Avni quoted why she had not visited the coffee shop.

"What are you up to these days? Have you managed to change your job?" asked the waiter, who knew about Avni's struggle with changing jobs. "Yes, I have joined as an assistant to the psychologist Adi." "You mean the great Adi?" The waiter interrupted. "I have been following his work and am a great fan of his," the waiter continued. Avni brightened, proud to work alongside such a renowned figure. "How is your back treating you?" Avni questioned, feeling joyous from being praised for her achievement of working with Adi.

"I replaced my motorbike with a car with a seat to support my sit bones," answered the man. "Congratulations, and you seem to be working out?" Avni asked about his body transformation. "Yeah, and that's how I know Adi sir," the man responded.

"Is he your gymmate?" grinned Avni.

"No, I have followed his work and suggestions on building a new routine. That's how I have joined the gym and followed a fitness regime," said the waiter.

"He lives downtown, right? And how come you work for him, which is far from here?" The waiter questioned. "Until a few months ago, he used to live there, but now he has moved and opened a clinic near this coffee place," answered Avni.

"Is it? That's great news. I must say that destiny has turned in your favor. Is everything going well with you?" Avni asked, referring to the waiter following Adi's work.

"I work here with dedication and sincerity. Though I live alone, I enjoy talking with customers. Yet I often feel sad that I lack close friends who can offer empathy, companionship, and support when needed. I have battled depression for a long time. I have been to multiple clinics, but found that psychiatrists today are not trained in psychotherapy. They're trained in what's called biological society, which fundamentally means altering the base of the brain by handing out prescriptions. I soon discovered that everything was a bandage, and there was no root cause analysis. I have been using stress medications with no luck. All the psychiatrists I have been to saw me for ten minutes and wrote a prescription. I came across Adi's work in psychology and have been following it for a long time, and it felt authentic. It took me a long time to realize that I was traumatized and that there were reasons for my struggles. But once I started looking for ways to heal, things began to change for me. I have changed my routine and have joined a gym. I am posting my fitness regime on social media every day. Don't you see them?" The enthusiastic waiter asked Avni.

"I do," Avni responded with a bright smile and patted him to boost his confidence in working towards healing himself. The waiter left after they both smiled at each other.

Although she was enjoying her work to the fullest as she started observing how to become a better person while treating patients with trauma and anxiety, her bond with Chetan was getting impacted.

Avni reminisced about the last time she met Chetan in the same coffee shop. It was a few months ago. Then, she excitedly asked him to meet her, hoping to share the big news that she had been invited for an interview to be a stenographer for the famous psychologist Dr. Adi. Though she hardly believed it when she received the letter, she needed Chetan's help in preparing for the interview.

Chetan walked into the cafe and saw Avni sitting at their usual table. He smiled and headed over. "I have some exciting news to share." Avni initiated the conversation as he took the seat.

"Ok, so shall we talk about your interview now?" Questioned the man of her dreams.

"How, on Earth, did you know that?" she asked in astonishment. "Your expression is quite evident. I can see the folded letter on the table, and a magazine of someone, I believe, is the person you will assist. I concluded without being conscious of the intermediate steps. Now, after your reply, I assume I was correct." Chetan pointed towards the open magazine about Adi and a folded call letter on the coffee table. However, he didn't remember Avni had applied for a stenographer position with Dr. Adi.

Chetan had a knack for deduction and analysis, not by luck, but he had developed the skill of deduction through years of long and patient study. Although amazed, she agreed with him as she understood his intellect nonverbally. She reminisced about how she was constantly shocked by his deductions during the initial phase of their relationship. Her interest in him and her curiosity about his aims in life gradually deepened.

"What have you been up to, Avni?" Chetan greeted her as he arrived at her table.

Avni, lost in thought, was suddenly pulled back to the present. Her heart leaped with joy at seeing him, sweeping away all her worries.

Avni jumped up from her chair as soon as she saw him, nearly knocking it over in her hurry. All the worries and overthinking she'd done during their time apart vanished instantly.

She hugged Chetan tightly, clinging to him like a lifeline. Wrapping her arms around his neck, she breathed in his familiar scent as a wave of relief washed over her. Tears of happiness pricked her eyes.

"I missed you so much," she murmured into his shoulder. After so long apart, the feeling of his strong arms around her again filled her with warmth and comfort. Her heart, which had felt heavy and uncertain, now lifted and soared. All was right in the world again now that he was here.

For a moment, time stood still. The cafe faded away as Avni focused only on the sound of Chetan's breath, the reassuring beat of his heart, and the safety of his embrace. Months of longing melted into this one perfect moment of reunion.

Slowly, reluctantly, Avni loosened her hold and stepped back to look at Chetan's face–that kind, handsome face that still had the power to take her breath away.

"I'm so glad you're here," she said, smiling at him through happy tears. Chetan squeezed her hand and smiled back. "I'm glad to be here," he replied.

Chetan's presence was enough to dispel Avni's troubled thoughts. In that moment, nothing existed but the pure joy of being together again. In his embrace, she was home. "You are as cute as you were," he said, kissing her forehead.

She realized then that love was not about schedules and scripts but fully embracing another's essence. Some things are more potent than clocks or calendars. Love was one of them. Two souls meant to touch, even if only for a moment, to share life's beauty and pain.

She gave him a short sketch of the adventures she had been having for all the past ten weeks and could hardly conclude them by the time her food arrived. The waiter acknowledged Chetan with a bright smile. Chetan greeted him and ordered for himself after receiving a warm greeting from the waiter. "Your social media feed is interesting," Chetan praised the waiter. The man grinned and left the couple with their privacy.

Although the pale look on Chetan's face told a different story, he empathized with Avni on every topic she touched upon. She observed him and said, "I may not be satisfied in admitting this, but I must, that you know every inch of me, but I don't know much about you. How are you? Please tell me how I can help you?"

Chetan looked at her with surprise. "Are you okay now?" she continued her question.

"Yes," answered Chetan.

"The last time I saw you, you were busy solving a crime that haunted your dreams and filled you with anxiety. You said you needed time to recover," Avni said, sorrow filling her voice.

She had worried about him constantly during their time

apart, imagining all the pain and turmoil the case had caused him. Seeing him now, her feelings rushed to the surface: relief, joy, and protectiveness.

"I thought of you often," she continued, reaching out to gently cup his cheek. "Wondering if you were eating, sleeping, taking care of yourself. It pained me to think of you suffering alone."

Her eyes searched his face, looking for any sign of the burden of that dark case. But all she saw was the man she loved, steady as a lighthouse amidst the chaos.

"I'm sorry I worried you," Chetan said softly. He clasped her hand and held it to his heart. "It was a difficult time, I won't deny that. But knowing you believed in me, that we'd see each other again...that gave me the strength to put one foot in front of the other."

Avni's heart swelled at his words. "Oh Chetan," she said, tears now falling freely. "I will always believe in you. And I will always be here when you're ready to share your burdens." She continued, "I'm sorry I let my work consume me."

Chetan smiled softly. "It's just who you are, following your passions. I understand." Avni sat across from Chetan, drinking at the sight of him.

"What was the case that troubled you so much? Do you mind discussing it?" Avni takes the moment to understand Chetan's current behavior before touching upon their marriage topic.

Chetan sighed deeply. "The case I just solved...it shook me to my core," he said.

"A mother murdered her 17-year-old son so he wouldn't inherit the family property. My usual logic and deductions failed me. Cases like that drain my mind and weaken my heart."

Avni saw the pain in Chetan's eyes and took his hand in hers.

He continued, "How can parents who bring us into this world also become the reason we leave it? It made me question everything."

His voice cracked with emotion. "I was emotionally exhausted. All I could think about was not to hurt that mother before handing her over to court. These few weeks have been a nightmare."

Avni's heart ached for Chetan. The horror of that case–a son betrayed by his own mother–weighed heavily on him.

"Oh Chetan," she said gently. "You have such a big heart; it's only natural that these things affect you deeply. But your capacity for compassion is also your greatest strength."

Chetan asked gently, "How was your day?" But Avni managed to see through his calm words. "Your eyes say more than your words," she replied.

She took his hand. "This is not a phase of admiring your positives and falling in love; we are in a phase where we have accepted each other. We're past that now."

Although he had bottled up the sadness and anger building inside him, he smiled for his girlfriend, not wanting to burden her. He intentionally avoided discussing his current mindset because he didn't want to trouble Avni.

They left the place and went to their respective homes.

THE CONVERSATIONS

Dr. Adi said confidently, "I will observe from the second chair today. I'd like you to lead this patient's session, Avni. This is his second visit, correct?"

Avni replied with nervousness, "Yes, but I'm not sure if I'm ready."

Dr. Adi was filled with confidence. "Remember our interview before you joined the practice? You had tremendous knowledge and passion then. Combine that with the practical exposure you've gained these past months."

A patient entered. Avni straightened her posture, radiating assurance. "Good morning," she said calmly. "I'm Dr. Avni. Please, have a seat." She shook the patient's hand firmly.

Avni sat across from her patient, listening carefully to his words. But something seemed off. The patient told her he was coping well, yet Avni sensed an undercurrent of tension in his voice.

She glanced around the room, taking in subtle details. The patient's foot tapped anxiously. His brow was furrowed ever so slightly. His eyes, though looking directly at Avni, seemed distant, unfocused.

These nonverbal cues told Avni that the patient, despite his assurances, was struggling. But how could she help if he refused to admit any trouble?

Avni took a deep breath and decided to trust her instincts. "Sir," she said gently, "you tell me you're coping well, yet your foot is tapping and your brow furrowed. This tells me something different. It's okay if you're struggling. You can talk to me about it."

The patient fell silent momentarily and looked at Adi, who signaled him to trust Avni with a quiet gesture. The patient then sighed. "You're right," he confessed. "I'm not coping well at all. I'm anxious all the time..." And so he began to open up, telling Avni about the troubles weighing on him.

"Thank you for trusting me," Avni said. The patient gave her a nod and smile, his foot finally still. The session was off to a good start.

He spoke confidently at first. The pain filled his voice gradually. "Growing up like I did, you expect people to yell and throw things. You don't know if you'll eat or get evicted. The currency meant nothing."

Avni listened closely to his words and subtle expressions. Through observing Adi keenly, she's learned that nonverbal cues help understand a patient's mental state during counseling. She asked gently, "What circumstances are you referring to?"

Tears filled the man's eyes. "My father killed himself under debt pressure when I was thirteen. I essentially raised myself with limited resources."

"I met a friend who got me into gambling. Once I was hooked, the law didn't scare me. I used people's trust and gambled away my money. Now I have become like my father."

"Why didn't the law scare you?" Avni asked.

"They could've locked me up. What's the difference? It's hard to find someone who can understand me. If I am gone, no one will miss me," he said hopelessly.

"Are you constantly anxious and stressed?"

"Yes, and my gambling addiction has ruined our family."

The doctor said solemnly, "Many people have traumatic childhood experiences that they don't know how to process. You are at the right place to unveil the process. So, trauma is not a bad thing that happens to you. It is just a response to what happened to you."

The man broke down sobbing. Years of pain and shame poured out. Avni handed him a tissue, her eyes filled with empathy and understanding. The man said shakily, "I just wanted to forget."

Avni replied, "I know. But you're not alone anymore. We're going to face this trauma together and heal from it." Hope lit up in his eyes through the tears. Avni's words, spoken with empathy and confidence, offered the first ray of light in his long darkness.

"Excellent," Adi praised Avni. The patiënt seemed confused as to how his trauma could be excellent. Adi, who understood the seriousness, realized that he had misspoken.

Apologizing to the patient, Avni continued. "What do you think when you gamble for fun?" "That's what destroyed me. However, it just takes the pain away. I tried building my dream so many times, I no longer have a dream."

"Do you immediately withdraw whenever you feel hurt from your relationships?" Avni realized the man's situation resembled Chetan's in some aspects. Adi observed Avni mixing the issue of Chetan with that of the gambler.

"Absolutely. So I don't have to feel those emotions when I am accountable for the relationship. Honestly, when the emotions are at high stake, I don't know what to do with them," answered the man. Adi asked Avni to continue taking notes. He took up the counseling session from there. Her pulse quickened as Adi took the seat.

"So you got disconnected from yourself. Do you know why we get disconnected?" Adi asked the man.

The patient picked nervously at his fingers and said,

"Because it's too painful to be ourselves?" They remained silent, listening and observing each other.

After a pause, the doctor responded gently. "You seem nervous just talking about this. When you disconnect from your feelings, you lose yourself."

The patient stuttered as Adi watched for cues beyond just his words. "I don't know why I'm so anxious and quiet all the time. I can't even cry to release my pain," the patient said as his hands moved restlessly.

Empathizing, the doctor said softly, "Once the heart grows too heavy with pain, people become silent. Completely silent."

The patient's eyes were welling with tears. "I feel trapped inside myself," he said quietly.

The doctor's voice filled with compassion. "I understand. But I can help guide you out of this trap." The patient looked up hopefully. "You can?"

The doctor said with confidence, "I recommend three more sessions. You'll see change by the end."

Relief filled the patient's eyes through his tears. After years of suffering in silence, the doctor's words–with empathy, understanding, and confidence–offered the first glimmer of hope that he could finally confront the pain weighing down his heart and find a way to let it out.

The doctor said gently, "This is the first step towards healing. You've already shown great courage by coming here today."

The patient wiped away a tear, glancing at the doctor with gratitude. For the first time in years, he felt seen, heard, and not alone in his suffering. Hope bloomed that he could finally rediscover himself amidst the silence and pain holding him captive for so long.

"Is it that Chetan immediately withdraws whenever he feels hurt from the relationship? Is he disconnected from himself as this gambler is?" Avni asked herself, not paying much attention to what was happening at the table.

She was in pain from being in a relationship that didn't know its future. She could not run away from it as she was madly in love. She could not understand why love entangled people. This love seemed to be the ultimate meaning of life, even if it was an incomprehensible book.

The doctor disturbed Avni's thought process and asked her what she would recommend doing in those three sessions. Avni responded confidently–

1. We help the patient identify and process his emotions in a safe environment. The session will allow the patient to feel and work through painful feelings with support. Meditation, journaling, and exercise teach the patient coping skills to manage anxiety and stress in a healthy way rather than escaping through gambling.

2. Forgiveness can aid in his emotional healing. The patient seems to feel quite ashamed, so we must ensure that he works on forgiving himself for his addictive behaviors.

3. Explaining how his experiences and behaviors fit common patterns can decrease shame and empower the patient to make changes. Setting goals for behavior change and new, healthier activities.

"Perfect, you have come a long way from your theoretical perspective to real solutions. I am confident you can carry on well in my absence, and I am so proud of you," said the doctor.

Avni was overwhelmed with the praise and happier that she could now help Chetan heal.

As Adi packed his things at the end of the day, Avni initiated a conversation, asking if he had thought about what to say to Rishi the following day.

Adi replied, "Life in prison is no joke, and I believe Rishi may have faced even harsher realities outside than he has here.

We should start by asking him about his difficult experiences while being incarcerated, and then show him the positive lives his peers lead after being granted parole. I understand that comparisons can be unhelpful sometimes, but showing him how others have improved their lives, both in the past and present, might help him trust us and encourage him to open up more. I'm sure this won't be an easy case to work through."

Avni reminisced about Chetan's similar situation and wanted to try the same method.

❖

Avni met Chetan again at the same cafe and continued their previous conversation.

Chetan sighed. "I know. This case and many other cases are taking a toll." He was referring to the case of a son betrayed by his own mother.

"Tell me how I can help." Avni squeezed his hand.

Chetan was quiet momentarily, realizing that real love holds your hand when life gets rough. "Just listen. That's all I need right now."

Chetan, who was dying for a listener, started to break down. "Do you know what's the hardest thing to do and that hurts the most? Crying with no sounds and tears. Although I look calm, content, and confident, there is a man who yearns for a listener in his life despite all the struggle, rage, pain, loneliness, family pressure, and depression."

"I love you for how empathetic you are," Chetan held her hand softly. She listened to him intently as Chetan spoke of the gruesome details, the sleepless nights, the doubt gnawing at his confidence.

"Solving the crimes where people die for a reason that I don't think is sensible is making me burn inside my body. Although life is a compromise between reality and perceived reality, I am done ignoring my feelings and accepting reality at every stage. This anxiety is killing me and keeping me awake. I need a break from my brain, the stress, and the pain." A brief pause.

"But I cannot quit. My mother, who raised me and my brother, taught us to be courageous in every situation. When I took up this job, I felt more confident when I helped people reveal the beauty of their existence that they had lost sight of because of trauma. Now it is not the case. I feel even more dejected thinking about letting down my people's confidence in me. My mother has raised us to be confident and content, not weak and cowardly. The feeling of incapability in handling the situations is destroying me. I tried not to think. Unfortunately, the silence was the killer, too. The only oil running my engine is my mother, who is very proud that her courageous son is out in the world giving justice to the people who have lost their lives for insensible, selfish reasons. However, if you could see it from my point of view, you would understand why it's so bad." Chetan put out his pain.

Avni noticed the inner pain no one talked about–Chetan, and his work. Although he helped people rediscover the beauty in life, he had lost it due to the trauma. He struggled more because his approach brought justice for victims. She recollected how Adi spoke from a place of empathy and understanding of the patient's pain. So, here to work through the trauma of other people, Chetan himself was traumatized. Realizing the pain of Chetan, Avni didn't know how to help her dear; often, the questions raised by Chetan made her think about how Adi could answer them. She hoped that Adi could help heal Chetan.

Avni did not try to fix or solve anything. When Chetan finished, Avni said, "Thank you for sharing this with me. I know it wasn't easy."

Chetan finally met her eyes. "You were right. Keeping it to

myself wasn't helping."

Avni looked at Chetan with worry. She saw him struggling but knew suggesting that he get help would never work.

Gently, she said, "Chetan, I can see now your work is affecting you deeply. You don't have to deal with this alone." Chetan sighed.

Why don't you share it with me whenever you feel low? That would help you." Avni said.

"I don't want to inflict my suffering on others," answered Chetan. She felt the pain in her chest after hearing the painful words from Chetan.

She reminisced about what Adi used to say: that there is so much that trauma makes us lose sight of the beauty we have. Working through trauma can teach us so much wisdom and can reveal the beauty of our existence that we lost sight of because of trauma. So, we must make the patient understand the importance of confronting the truth.

Avni consoled Chetan, saying, "We're all in this together. You have nothing to be ashamed of. Anxiety is increasingly common these days. Professional help can make a huge difference."

"I feel ashamed that I am also a part of those alone people who are sufficiently anxious to be diagnosed," said Chetan.

"We are here for you. Don't worry. This is the only place where they don't see what's wrong with people; instead, they see what happened to people," consoled Avni, referring to Adi's clinic.

Chetan responded gently, "Avni, I know you want to help. But as much as I value your advice and care, I'm not sure it would have the same impact coming from someone close to me. You know me too well on an emotional level for your perspective to feel truly objective. Have you ever thought if you would be able to see me as one of your patients walking in your door asking for help?"

She could not bear the thought of Chetan speaking about his weakness in front of Adi and herself in the treatment room. Still, she pushed her tone, "I can try."

Chetan disagreed. He accepted the truth that he couldn't disclose his insecurities to any other person, and definitely not to a stranger, who was Adi.

"Why don't your parents get us married off so that I can take care of you with all my strength?" She lightly touched upon the sensitive topic they both wanted but never discussed.

The waiter interrupted again to remind them that it was closing time. Avni asked Chetan to accompany her to her home. They both continued their soul talks and reached home late at midnight. She hugged him again, gently this time, holding him close and breathing in the life and light that radiated from this incredible man she loved so much. Chetan hugged her closely before leaving the place.

For now, all he needed was Avni's shoulders to rely on and a warm embrace. They could be his healing at the moment.

Avni felt bad that the man who had always filled her with courage was in such a state that she had to ask him to consult the doctor for professional help. She was afraid she could not leave him like that, as it would not be right, owing to his profession. If his anxiety peaked, it could be harmful to the people around him.

Her mind was filled with the question–How can I help him?

Avni didn't have an answer for two reasons; One, she could not see treating Chetan without her clouded judgment. Two, she wasn't professional enough to deal with him alone. Though she accurately diagnosed conditions, her practical experience remained limited as she was still learning.

Over time, with enough practical experience, Avni might gain the confidence and skills to treat some patients independently. However, she would likely continue consulting with Adi for complex cases. She was eager now to gain that exposure so that she could heal Chetan herself professionally.

❖

Avni found herself struggling to fall asleep. Although her eyes begged her to sleep, she was stuck in the silent war between her heart and mind. Lying in her bed, her thoughts drifted to how destiny had transformed Chetan's once confident self into someone now filled with insecurity, despite his work serving justice to society.

She reminisced when a few months ago, Chetan met Avni with a call letter in the coffee shop.

"What else do you know about him?" asked Chetan, pulling the magazine towards him.

"He has lived in the downtown area his whole life. He's in his late 50s. He's extremely wealthy. It's unclear what prompted him to open this clinic in our city. The clinic has only been open a few months and is actively seeking an assistant. He has a master's degree from London. Due to his skill in psychology, putting Adi's name on any building attracts many patients."

Avni asked, "How should I handle him in the interview since he is good at quickly analyzing people? If I'm not mistaken, he will know within 30 seconds if a person is suitable for the job. How can I impress him in those 30 seconds? Tell me anything apart from making strong eye contact, firm handshake, confident voice, smile, positive body language, to make an impression in an interview."

Chetan was busy looking at Adi's posts and pictures in the magazine and said, "I should learn from you how to crack an interview." Referring to the traits she had put before him.

He continued, "However, I think I have your answer. You are lucky that I have crossed paths with him recently, which could help you land the job. In height, he was rather over six feet and so excessively lean. As for myself, even your Adi sir does seem considerably taller due to his lean body. His eyes were sharp, and his thin nose gave his whole expression an air of alertness and decision-making. His chin, too, had the prominence which marked the man's determination."

"Why did he live downtown when he is that popular?"

"Maybe he is comfortable there, or the place must be significant to him."

"Why did he move to the city at this age? Is it regarding his kids' studies? The magazine says that he doesn't have any."

"It must be more relevant to cities than downtowns, so mostly medical."

"Someone he is close to must be going through some serious medical need that allowed him to move back to the city."

"Who might it be? Mother? Wife? Father?"

"It cannot be anyone apart from the above, as we rarely care to move out of our comfort zone if it is for anyone else."

"I probably think it must be mostly his wife or mother."

"How can you be so sure about the care home?"

"Looking at this picture," Chetan pointed to a picture of Adi in front of a car.

"Have you seen this car?"

"Yes! I went to pick up my family from a care home, which is ten minutes away from Adi's clinic. The number plate is the same. All these conclude that he has moved here to take care of someone who has joined a care service." Chetan said.

The whole train of thought did not occupy a minute. So here, within a minute of looking at a picture, Chetan had concluded the reason. He always looked for something new every time, which enabled him to be skillful in the science of deduction. "It is simple enough as you explain it. So what should be my opening statement in the interview tomorrow?" she asked, smilingly.

They spoke about various states of mind as they understood the science behind it, which was interesting. She enjoyed every conversation with Chetan, and her respect for his powers of analysis increased wondrously.

She felt equally warm whenever she saw this emotional side of him, but never imagined it would come down to this situation. It is true that when we can no longer change a situation, we are challenged to change ourselves.

She wondered if he knew that whenever the darkness threatened to overwhelm him again, she would be there to light his way. Would he be able to convince himself to get married?

Slowly, the thought of being competent for marriage had been replaced by simply being content with each other. Now, there was only healing, hope, and a love that knew no bounds. The nightmares and anxiety had the power to shatter many lives, and Chetan was no exception.

Maybe this was how love worked. When you love someone, you love them through all moods and circumstances. We get embraced with our flaws and get noticed for our weakest achievements.

"I will try to see what I can do for Chetan." She said to herself and fell asleep thinking of ways to help him.

THE INVESTIGATION DRAMA

It had been a week since Lalit's mysterious murder, yet Chetan still struggled to make sense of the incomplete evidence, which provided little insight. Chetan, often quick to understand the evidence and read crime scenes, struggled due to personal problems.

Most parameters recovered were either incomplete or irrelevant. Footprints and tire tracks were misleading, as it was a public area. The blood spatter matched Lalit's, but there were no other samples. The weapon seemed unclear; however, iron rods, broken glass, and sharp objects were photographed at the scene.

Chetan requested that Lalit's office provide him with the cases Lalit had been working on or had worked on in the past to draw a suspect list. However, as the work associated with Lalit was linked to the financial obligations and due to client confidentiality, the company refused to disclose any information.

The contact list on the phone acquired from the crime scene didn't contain any contacts related to his profession; all of them were of Lalit's friends and relatives. He could not believe that Lalit had no professional contacts on his mobile. So, the mobile also yielded no leads.

Chetan picked the photographs taken from the crime scene and observed that the phone in his hand was taken from a backpack in the trunk of Lalit's car. However, Lalit had a mobile in his hand while entering the gym, which Chetan confirmed with the surveillance footage collected from the gym.

How come Lalit went to his car, put back his phone, and went to the crime scene, which was about 300 yards from his car? The autopsy confirmed that he had been murdered 10 minutes from the time he left the gym, which pointed to Lalit not having enough time to put the phone in his backpack. Since the crime scene and the car were far away from each other.

Either the murderer had kept the phone, which meant the murderer was someone known to him, or this wasn't his primary phone. Although the device resembled the one he was been seen carrying in the CCTV footage, there appeared to be a discrepancy. If he had carried it with him while being strangled, there should have been visible external damage. On the other hand, if he had left it in the trunk before meeting the murderer at the crime scene, then this couldn't have been the phone he was seen with.

The only plausible explanation was that Lalit had one phone in his hand when he entered the gym, but a different phone was later found in the trunk of his car. However, the autopsy revealed he died just 10 minutes after leaving the gym—far too little time to have returned the phone to the car, making this the only logical conclusion.

Chetan dialed Lalit's family and understood he had two similar phones. He requested them to send details of the other phone. So came the question–where was the second phone? There was no other phone on the body. There was no phone in the trunk, and Lalit would not have left his phone carelessly owing to the sensitive information that it carried. He had a long list of big-shot clients with financial obligations that no one else should have known. Either the murderer had the phone, or, coincidentally, he must have lost the phone. Both led Chetan to go close to the murderer.

The autopsy provided a detailed and objective analysis of the cause and manner of death. So Chetan thoroughly reviewed the physical evidence collected from the crime scene again. The forensic pathologist collected a small glass piece from the throat of the deceased. The piece belonged to the weapon used to slit Lalit's throat. The medical examiner also confirmed that the slit was very sharp so that a colder glass might have been used rather than a dry one.

Of all the photographs collected that held sharp objects, he found pieces of a glass bottle. He took out an evidence bag containing pieces of glass. His team put together the glass pieces like a jigsaw puzzle and inferred the bottle to be a famous soda brand sold in the market. The next step–how to get to the culprit using the clue of this bottle?

It was a challenging task. They found hundreds roaming around holding a soda bottle in their hands. However, even the most remarkable criminals can make the slightest errors they are unaware of. Here, the mistake was using that bottle to slit the throat. Chetan now had: the time of death, the murder weapon.

Additionally, the weapon must be chilled, meaning it must have been bought just before the murder. So, how many stores nearby sold that brand of soda? It was summertime, meaning the chilliness wouldn't last long, allowing the search area to be reduced.

The team searched the entire surroundings and every shop that sold sodas. Chetan shortlisted the nearest marts selling sodas and checked all photographic evidence from nearby cameras that could help identify suspects in the provided timeline of events. It took almost a week. After investing so much effort, they had gotten a list of people who had purchased the bottles at the mentioned timelines near the gym area. Chetan drove all the informers on the search to find the people on the suspects' list. The search had begun.

One of his search operator mates traced Lalit's phone in the nearby bush, where the murderer must have thrown it. Being a criminologist, Chetan had to think from a criminal's point of view on why the murderer had done this, also analyzing patterns so that the crime would not be repeated in the future. But his current mental state didn't allow him to understand himself; thinking through someone else's mind was almost impossible.

Chetan's focus became sharp as he retrieved Lalit's work contacts from the recovered mobile phone. His mind raced, piecing together each suspect on the list with clues from Lalit's call logs. After thoroughly scrutinizing the data, Chetan ticked off the names of those who seemed innocent.

Chetan felt a jolt of shock as he examined one particular call log. Lalit had spoken with Chetan's mother on the day of the murder for a lengthy two hours.

Chetan hastily started dialing his mother, his heart pounding. Coincidentally, he received a call from his mother before he could dial. She informed him about his brother's disappearance from the day before.

Chetan felt as though the floor was dropping from beneath him. He abruptly ended the call and redialed Vinay's number with trembling fingers. It didn't connect.

Sweat beaded on Chetan's forehead as disturbing scenarios flashed through his mind. A kidnapping? Foul play? What did Lalit talk to his mother about during their two-hour call? How come his brother Vinay went missing?

The harrowing revelations came too fast for Chetan to process rationally. His thoughts swirled into a panic as his hands shook uncontrollably and his heart pounded out of control. He suddenly felt like his heart was racing, and he couldn't catch his breath. He got dizzy, started sweating, and thought he must escape. These symptoms peaked within 10 minutes and gradually subsided over the next few minutes. This was the first time he had experienced a panic attack. He felt like he was losing control of himself.

A couple of days passed by. Chetan ignored Avni's calls, preoccupied with finding his missing brother and deeply embarrassed by his emotional confession. Avni was concerned, but couldn't leave her work to be with him. She had grown to understand patients' emotions, but not Chetan's.

Avni hoped learning about Chetan's childhood would provide insight into his behavior. She contacted his mother, Indira, hoping to gain some perspective. This was when Indira shared that Chetan had been searching for his missing brother, Vinay.

Avni froze, stunned into silence. She had spoken to Vinay just days ago! To avoid confusing Indira with this information, Avni quickly ended the call.

A cold thrill of unease rippled through her. Her heart raced as she texted Chetan–she needed to see him immediately, in person. He didn't reply, although he had seen her text.

❖

"I stepped through the heavy iron doors of the prison 25 years ago; I can still feel the sound echoing." Rishi started confessing while Avni made notes, and Adi was keen on observing his gestures.

"The first few months were the hardest. I understood the reality of my situation, battling feelings of despair and isolation. Surrounded by hardened criminals, I felt like an outsider. The prison's environment was harsh, and the threat of violence was ever-present."

"Loneliness consumed me as I lost contact with friends and

family. I missed birthdays, weddings, and the simple joy of sharing a meal with loved ones. Each day felt like an eternity. I was assaulted physically and mentally. There was never a day when I didn't feel like taking my life."

"As time passed, I realized I had two choices: succumb to despair or find a way to survive. I began attending educational programs offered within the prison. These classes became a lifeline, allowing me to focus on self-improvement."

"Amidst the bleakness, I found camaraderie with a small group of inmates who shared similar aspirations. They motivated each other, discussing books and dreams of a better future. This sense of community helped me combat the pervasive loneliness that haunted me."

"The small group of mine went away by parole and within no time committed suicide one by one as they had challenges in getting used to society. They couldn't bear being mistreated and discriminated against by society. I don't have anyone out there for me, and I cannot relive my initial days in prison. So please leave me alone." Rishi pleaded with the doctors.

Both doctors left the prison.

THE PATH TOWARDS HEALING

The next morning at Dr. Adi's office, Avni assisted and supported him with work, showing utmost professionalism. She scheduled appointments, actively listened while patients described their conditions, and concisely briefed Dr. Adi before each patient arrived.

Avni informed Dr. Adi that he had a patient scheduled in 30 minutes. Several patients required therapy sessions once every two weeks, while others needed sessions once a month. Dr. Adi saw at least three patients daily, so he relied on Avni's meticulous record-keeping to recall each patient's history, prior prescriptions, and what transpired during their last session. Avni's well-organized briefings allowed Dr. Adi to accurately diagnose and treat each patient based on the information obtained while scheduling the appointment. Avni's thorough professionalism and organizational skills were essential to Dr. Adi's practice.

Dr. Adi looked up from his notebook, removing his glasses as he spoke to Avni. "The next patient, is she a regular or new client?"

Avni confidently responded, "Yes, doctor, she has been seeing you for the last three sessions." She stated, "She came to you seeking relief from anxiety, panic attacks, and phobias."

Avni continued her summary in a calm, measured tone. "She mentioned that these symptoms have troubled her since childhood but have worsened noticeably in recent months. Before initiating therapy here, she was nearly paralyzed due to intense emotions. However, the traditional therapeutic techniques you have employed seem to be helping her gain mastery over her symptoms."

Dr. Adi nodded thoughtfully as Avni spoke, stroking his chin. "And can you remind me, what triggered her panic and anxiety in the first place?"

"I am reading the notes," said Avni. She reminisced about the day while she went through her notes.

Dhwani's voice cracked as she spoke. "My husband and I had always dreamed of a big family. So when I found out I was pregnant last summer, we were over the moon." She wiped a tear from her cheek. "This was a long-planned pregnancy."

"But during the 12-week ultrasound, doctors discovered our baby had an anencephalic cyst–the baby's organs were forming outside its body." She paused, as pain etched on her face. "The day this news came to me was the most devastating day of my life. The doctors said our baby wouldn't survive, even with intensive care."

She breathed shakily. "I was told I could lose my life. At 19 weeks, we made the agonizing decision to terminate the pregnancy." Her voice broke. "It was the only choice to save myself and give our baby the dignity it deserved. Carrying the baby to full term would have only meant burying us both."

Tears flowed freely now. "The abortion was physically and emotionally traumatic." She covered her face. "When I came home, I fell into the lowest point of my life. I couldn't get out of bed, eat, or focus on work. It felt like I'd lost a part of myself. Everything I was afraid of happening had just happened in weeks."

She looked up; a sob escaped her lips. "And then, just months after the abortion, my husband died in a car accident. It pushed me into hell."

"The last thing I said to my husband was in anger during an argument. I'll never be happy with those final words."

Composing herself, she said, "It cost me my husband's death for me to learn this valuable lesson: talk to people nicely, we don't know what awaits us in the future, you should be happy with the last thing you've said to someone."

As Avni reviewed Dhwani's file, the receptionist knocked on the door to inform them that Dhwani had been waiting in the lobby. Dr. Adi gestured to send Dhwani in after a brief delay.

Dr. Adi turned to Avni and said, "What do you think would most benefit a person suffering as Dhwani is?"

Dr. Adi continued, "I believe empathy through a relatable story could provide solace. We must show sincere empathy and insight, allowing Dhwani to express herself fully."

Shortly after, Dhwani entered the office. Dr. Adi and Avni greeted her professionally. "Good morning, Dhwani! You look confident."

Dr. Adi said, "Dhwani, please know that we are your doctors, and we hope to create a safe space for you to share your experiences."

Dhwani's voice cracked as she spoke. "I was confident until I saw a father walking with his healthy baby through the hospital doors."

Tears welled up in her eyes. "You know thousands of women die yearly due to congenital disabilities. But safe abortion is essential for women's health, which you did," Dr. Adi consoled.

"Suffering is personal, but it shouldn't rule the life you lead or want to lead." Hopelessly, Dhwani cried, "I see no reason to live. I constantly have suicidal thoughts. I feel like I'm in a dark room with no light. My eyes cannot see a colorful life ahead."

"There is so much excitement in life to savor," the doctor

motivated.

Her voice trembled. "My tears don't allow me to find excitement in life."

The doctor consoled, "Your pain is immense. But your will to live remains, else you wouldn't have come here today."

Dhwani sobbed, "I came because I didn't know where else to go. My pain consumes me."

The doctor paused for a moment and prepared his words before speaking. "Your pain does not define you. And you are not alone in this."

Dhwani shook, overwhelmed with grief. "I feel so alone." The doctor assured, "I know. But we are here with you. We will walk with you into the light, little by little again."

The doctor spoke gently. "This emptiness has its roots in your childhood." Dhwani looked at him, confused.

The doctor asked softly, "Shall we discuss more about the activities from your childhood?"

Dhwani sadly spoke, "I had a difficult one. My parents struggled with their own issues. They often neglected me, and I ended up feeling lonely and lost."

"As an adult, I found joy volunteering at an animal shelter. I loved feeding, comforting, and playing with the rescued dogs and cats. Before our marriage, my husband noticed for the first time how patient I was."

Her voice wavered as she recalled, "That was our third meeting. He said 'You have a gift for caring for others. I want to raise my kids in a safe environment like you create.' I was shocked the moment he proposed to me. 'You think so?' I asked. He replied, 'I know so. The way you comfort these animals, it's like you understand their need for love and security on a deep level.'"

Dhwani paused and cried as she said, "We were married and happy...until the tragedy."

The doctor said, "I think I understand. You never had any care as a child, so you gave that care to animals, healing yourself too."

Dhwani let out a small smile through her tears. "You're right," she whispered. "I wanted to give my child the love I craved as a child."

"That's often how it works. Those who needed care the most when they were young tend to give the most care as adults. You're a nurturer, Dhwani. Don't ever forget that." The doctor motivated her. "You have so much love to give. In time, you'll find peace again."

Dhwani's tears now carried a glimmer of hope.

Avni, who was busy taking notes, stopped momentarily to check if this could help Chetan in any way possible.

The doctor continued the conversation by referring to the animal shelter, "And you should be grateful to have found a place where you can nurture others while nurturing yourself. Why don't you rejoin the shelter to progress in life?"

The woman wiped tears from her cheeks as she struggled to hold back more. "How can I find gratitude when I couldn't even care for my baby and husband?" Immense doubt clouded her.

The therapy sessions helped Dhwani process her grief and trauma. Speaking about her experiences provided some relief, yet she still lacked the confidence to face life.

The doctor said gently, "Let me share a window into my own trauma. Do you believe that once I, along with my wife, decided to end our lives?"

He continued, "Once, my wife and I conceived a baby when we were too young and unready. After much discussion, we chose to give up the baby through adoption, not abortion."

The doctor's voice turned somber. "We were in London then, and that trimester was tough. We felt guilty." He glanced at Dhwani and Avni's shocked expressions but pressed on.

"We never learned the baby's gender or fate. Giving up that child ended our hopes for more kids, through birth or adoption."

The doctor spoke softly. "Suffering is personal, yet some find strength in it. Being strong doesn't mean that you're numb to pain. Instead, you find ways to deal with it. Although my wife is in her last stages of life, she never had any thoughts about the baby, nor any guilt surrounding it. That's the power of facing the truth."

He looked at Dhwani and said, "Your loss is permanent, but mine isn't. I don't mean to compare our losses, but there can be life even after the worst fears and sufferings."

Silence filled the room. Determination filled Dhwani's tearful eyes. She had found relief in sharing her pain and hope in the doctor's story of moving beyond trauma to create meaning. Dhwani spoke in a small voice. "You're right. I can find hope again, in time."

The doctor smiled. "One day at a time. You've taken the first steps already."

"What comforts you to come out of pain?" The doctor questioned her after a brief pause.

"I have been taking alcohol lately," she responded.

"You have to let your feelings come out. Please do not suppress them and make it worse by surrendering yourself to alcohol. It can result in other problems. It's important to take care of yourself by keeping a normal lifestyle."

"Remember that returning to how you felt before may take some time. If your distress continues or you face trouble managing your feelings, you can always contact me. However, before you leave, I would like to perform a session that can help you confront yourself with the truth." The doctor concluded.

Both Dhwani and Adi moved into the therapy room. Avni noted everything that happened and felt more confident about her career in this department, for she was trained under a master like Adi. However, she struggled to gain the confidence to help Chetan by herself.

The doctor informed Avni that though Dhwani would always grieve for her child, the therapy sessions were helping her develop positive ways to manage her emotions. Dhwani was making progress. Positive self-talk would be the way forward for her.

Avni questioned the doctor further. "But that story you told, was any of it true?"

The doctor replied, "No, that was just an example to illustrate how trauma affects people."

He explained, "Tragedies impact individuals in different ways. Some react immediately, while others' responses emerge later. People may feel fearful, relive past trauma, or struggle with a sense of loss, helplessness, or numbness."

"We have to help them mitigate that very nature by showing them that there is life after the pain. Death is not the biggest loss in life. The biggest loss is when a part of you dies inside while you are still alive. So, we have to take such steps in our profession," said the doctor.

"You misguided her?" Avni asked the question.

The doctor responded, "You're right, I did. When patients are fragile, we must provide empathy, not just clinical perspectives."

The doctor continued, "Talking about their experiences and receiving support from loved ones can help immensely. However, comparing stories with acquaintances like me may often lead to motivation."

Avni agreed, "You're right. Dhwani needs time and empathy right now."

"When Dhwani understands that I don't have kids and my wife is in the hospital, she gets to know that there are people who face worse than what she is going through. Once motivated,

Dhwani is determined to heal and move forward to focus on the future she and her husband want to build together. Once she comes out of her grief by facing her truth, my lie won't matter anymore."

"As the conversation continues, share your own experiences and memories related to the topic. This can help create a sense of connection and mutual understanding. Please be aware that avoiding judgment or criticism is essential while talking about past events. Instead, focus on understanding the other person's perspective and experiences."

The doctor told Avni, "We must assure patients that we understand their pain and are here to support their recovery journey."

While Avni was happy about Dhwani's improving mental health, she was lost in deep thoughts about Chetan. She had never seen him in such an emotional state. Her mind was actively considering what to say to empathize with him, yet she was aware that Chetan knew her inside out. She could not lie or quote anecdotes to sound convincing.

Adi, observing Avni lost in thought, checked on her. Avni acknowledged she was okay. She said, "We don't understand the strength of a relationship until suffering tests it."

Upon hearing this, Adi enquired, "Is everything okay with you and Chetan?"

Avni shook her head no and recalled the incident at the coffee shop. After narrating the event, she told Adi that she had asked Chetan to visit the clinic, but he refused.

"It seems something is dangerous with how you have explained his symptoms. Did he mention any physical symptoms or panic attacks?" The doctor asked. "No," Avni responded.

The doctor advised, "Professional help works best when the patient is receptive. Right timing is the key."

"Bring him when you feel it's the right time for him to heal from his pain, not when he thinks he can heal himself. Pain can make familiar routines feel unsafe. Let him get diverted with his routine."

Avni cared deeply for Chetan and wanted to ease his pain, but she had been approaching the situation from her perspective as a loved one and had been impulsive in finding the solution. However, as a doctor, she had to consider Chetan's perspective and healing pace.

"Avni, as your doctor and friend, I must remind you that while our medical skills help others, they can also make us hesitate to seek help for ourselves or our loved ones," the doctor said.

Avni realized the doctor was right. She had been so focused on helping Chetan that she failed to consider the right timing. Chetan's reluctance for professional help did not necessarily mean he didn't need it, but he was not yet ready. Avni, pushing the issue, risked damaging their relationship.

"I don't want Chetan to hate me while I try to force him to seek help," Avni said.

"Some hearts do not know how to hate, no matter how much they have been wronged. I am speaking from the perspective of what my eyes saw through yours whenever you speak about Chetan." The doctor praised the bond by describing Chetan's perceived character.

Avni thanked the doctor for the wise advice and reassurance. She decided to approach Chetan with more empathy and care, bringing him help when he felt ready. For now, she would simply listen and be present for him as a loving partner. The receptionist opened the door, informing Adi and Avni that their next patient was ready. Adi asked her to allow the patient in.

THE THREADS

While Chetan had solved many horrific cases, he had never felt afraid during investigations, but investigating his missing brother and the mysterious connection of his mother with Lalit filled Chetan with terror.

He was experiencing the worst feeling ever. He had no one to confide in, and the constant fear was slowly eating him.

Chetan searched desperately for his brother in many places but could not find him. He remained in constant touch with his mother, updating her on his search, but could not summon the courage to ask her about Lalit.

Chetan was driving on the highway when a wave of intense fear overcame him. His hands started trembling, and he struggled to focus on the road. He pulled over, and the symptoms continued for about 15 minutes before slowly fading.

Subconsciously, many terrifying thoughts ran through his mind. Every lead he had pursued up to this point indicated that something terrible was imminent. He desperately hoped that his brother would remain safe and unharmed.

With a heavy sigh, Chetan continued driving. The fear and helplessness threatened to overwhelm him, yet he steeled himself, squaring his shoulders with determination. He would find his brother, whatever it took.

Chetan received a phone call; a constable informed him that Vinay's lifeless body had been discovered in an abandoned house on their street. The grim news shook Chetan to his core. In shock and horror, he hurriedly drove to the scene.

However, Chetan parked roughly 100 meters away, unable to muster the strength to go closer. Instead of entering the house, he examined the surroundings.

The house seemed empty, with no CCTV cameras. An alley perpendicular to the main road led to it. The main road was about 150 meters away, with tall trees lining both sides of the alley. The place was damp from the previous night's rain.

Chetan looked up and down the pavement, steadily at the ground, sky, opposite alley, and house fencing. He examined the ground leading from the gate to the entrance. He stopped multiple times, observing everything.

The impatient constable was unwilling to wait, interrupting Chetan repeatedly to hand over the primary details. But Chetan remained unfazed.

Unfortunately, there were many footprints of differing sizes in the wet soil. This could have been a significant breakthrough in identifying those who accompanied Vinay.

Chetan observed the constable's foot size and then asked how he arrived. The constable pointed to his motorcycle parked outside the gate next to a tree.

Chetan questioned, "How did you know a body was here to recover?"

The constable explained, "While on patrol this morning, I noticed the gate was open in an unusual manner. I've patrolled this area for so long, I sensed something was wrong with the abandoned house."

He continued, "So I entered and found Vinay's body. I immediately informed my subordinates, who directed me to your agency, since you've been looking for Vinay."

Chetan visualized the constable discovering the gruesome scene: entering the decrepit house, finding Vinay's lifeless form, and calling for help.

Chetan queried, "What was the state of the body when you found it?"

The constable described the body's position and any visible wounds or signs of struggle.

Chetan scanned the surroundings again, analyzing every detail: the disturbed ground outside the gate, indentations in the muddy alley, and drapes shifting slightly in the morning breeze.

His mind raced, piecing clues together into a horrific picture of Vinay's last moments. He demanded, "Who else has been inside since you found the body?" The constable admitted that other officers had also entered.

Chetan grimly realized that potential evidence might have been compromised. But he remained determined, re-examining the scene with a keen eye and sharp mind, vowing to bring Vinay's killers to justice, no matter what clues might have been lost.

Inside, Chetan found Vinay's helpless body on the bare furniture. Chetan became emotionally unstable, struggling to look at his brother's motionless figure with sightless eyes staring blankly at the ceiling. Vinay's limbs were interlocked, indicating a painful death.

'How did he end up here?' Chetan thought to himself. The expression on Vinay's face was neutral, but his body was rigid.

Though grief threatened to overwhelm him, Chetan's detective instincts kicked in as he observed the scene. His mind started working faster than usual, desperation energizing his thoughts.

He noticed there had been no robbery, nor any evidence as to how Vinay met his death. There were no wounds, no signs of trauma. Yet the rigid limbs and open, vacant eyes indicated Vinay did not die peacefully.

Tears welled up in Chetan's eyes as he gazed at his brother's still form. He recalled Vinay's smile, infectious laugh, and hands patting him on the back. Yet those memories now seemed forever out of reach, trapped behind Vinay's face's cold, lifeless mask.

The grief threatened to consume Chetan completely. But he steeled himself, squaring his shoulders with determination. He would bring Vinay's killers to justice, giving his brother's soul the peace in death it was denied in life. Chetan investigated the scene with that resolution, desperately searching for clues through his tears.

The abandoned house would have been a convenient location for a crime to occur unseen. There were marks of a couple of droplets of blood, but there was no wound upon the person, except the area below the body, which looked extra clean despite the surrounding area being dusty.

Chetan deduced that Vinay was strangled on the floor before passing away. The constable continued the proceedings as Chetan did his job. He observed that all the other rooms in the building had been closed for months. The solitary window was so dirty that the light was hazy and uncertain, giving a dull gray tinge to everything, which was intensified by the thick layer of dust that coated the whole apartment.

He collected a sample of blood droplets and observed that the odor of the perfume was different, the one on the body, the one on the shoulders, and the one on the neck. When he observed closely, he could see a thin syringe mark on his neck. It could be that Vinay might be using a narcotic substance, or he might have been injected with something that killed him. He knew that his brother wasn't into any of the narcotics stuff. He observed every inch of the body and informed the constable to take the body to the mortuary.

The key deductions that Chetan made based on what he observed at the crime scene included the footprints, blood droplets, perfume smells, syringe marks, Vinay's body, and its state and position. All these clues pointed to Vinay being accompanied by multiple people and likely being strangled and/or injected with a substance that caused his death.

Even a thorough search of the abandoned house where Vinay's body was discovered didn't reveal any clues that pointed to the cause and circumstances of his death. There was no evidence of foul play, drugs, medical items, or hazards that could provide more information.

From the evidence collected and/or crime scene study, Chetan couldn't gather concrete leads on who the other people accompanying Vinay might be. His deductions focused more on what happened to Vinay than on identifying specific suspects.

He gathered all his courage to call his mom to inform her about his brother's death. He didn't want to trouble her with Lalit's case yet; however, his mind wasn't calm. Indira, the mother of two, reached the spot and was inconsolable after seeing her son's motionless body. He disconnected the call he received from Avni while consoling his mother. He remembered Avni's text stating that she had spoken with Vinay the day before. Avni could be the last one with whom Vinay might have spoken.

For years, Chetan had avoided confronting his fears. Now, those fears had become his limitations. He couldn't think logically as his mind was flooded with rage over his brother's murder. He never understood his mother when she told him to rise above the pain and seek justice if his family suffered. Those words rang true now that his brother was murdered.

❖

Avni lay in her bed, wide awake and clouded with a fury of thoughts. She thought of Chetan and decided to speak with his mother about him.

Anxiety gripped her as she considered contacting Indira. She was embarrassed due to their previous conversation about marriage with Chetan, as they had asked for some time, which wasn't up yet, and she couldn't figure out how to handle the situation after discovering Vinay's disappearance.

Her thoughts drifted back to the day of her interview. Her conversation with Adi about handling difficult situations now echoed Chetan's plight. If she remained silent, would she be encouraging Chetan's unhealthy behavior? But confronting Indira felt intrusive and risky. What if the conversation didn't turn out to be fruitful, but instead more problematic?

The uncertainty kept her awake, possibilities crowding her mind–each scenario making her more anxious than the previous one.

Avni's heart ached with concern for Chetan, yet reaching out to his mother felt immature. Her hand trembled slightly as she thought of calling Indira.

Indecision racked Avni as the early hours of the morning passed. Should she have warned Indira of possible trouble? Or have respected Chetan and Indira's privacy?

Unable to quiet her anxious thoughts, Avni rose from the bed. Pacing the room, various scenarios plagued her. Each decision carried risks to her relationship with Chetan.

But inaction might worsen Chetan's current situation.

Unable to settle on the right course of action, Avni knew one thing – staying silent was no longer an option. She reminisced about her interview with Adi a few months ago.

❖

Avni entered the interview room while Adi rested on his chair.

She walked towards him, shaking his hand rather enthusiastically than professionally. "You seem confident and content," said the wise man before gesturing to a seat. Her heartbeat quickened as she sat. "How are you?" He asked kindly.

"I… I am mm good, thanks," nervousness overcame her as she said the words.

Avni eagerly awaited the opportunity to impress Adi, the eminent psychologist she had admired for years. When he asked her, "What do you know about me?", she recounted various facts from the magazine articles she had read about him.

She was not expecting it to be the first question, but it did not surprise her as this was expected from him. Although she didn't have a photographic memory, she had gone through the magazine enough to remember every detail of him, which she articulated to Adi. Along with the facts, she listed the deductions made by Chetan for his family member being in the care service.

"Interesting! We can make a good team," said the man while her heart skipped a beat, assuming she had crossed the first 30 seconds on a positive note. "My wife is battling cancer, which left me no choice but to move here. Yes, I have joined her in the nearest health care service." Adi spilled the facts referring to the deduction about his current state.

"I love you, Chetan," the voice in her mind thanked him for the help.

"I understand, sir, and I feel my credentials suit me to handle cases swiftly," she tried to emphasize her strengths for the job opportunity.

"I am impressed with your research about the job and your control over the science of deduction. Now, let me ask you a few questions." He said to Avni.

"What do you think about trauma?"

"Battling a war with the unknown," She replied. Silence set in. She explained, "What I have identified with for the longest time is that I tend to believe that people who go through rough family childhoods swing either way. They either want to start a family because they don't want to repeat their parents' mistakes or go the other direction."

"Any treatment or medication? How do you heal?" The doctor questioned Avni.

"Every traumatized person wants to be a better person. The truth is that trauma can be healed, reversed, or transformed. We must reach that nerve in the brain to start with. There is no single pill to provide the solution. Confrontation is the solution."

"Confrontation with?" Adi interrupted in between. She continued, "Confrontation with one's darkest fears that are deeply held, firmly rooted as beliefs. It is the hardest part."

"Does it work every time?" He continued his questions.

"Not every time. If the conventional mechanism doesn't suit, then there are a few methods like hypnotism, the use of psychedelic drugs that can induce visions and deep experiences." Avni responded.

Adi rubbed his hands in a self-satisfied way. "Any thoughts on anxiety?" Adi continued with his questions. The expression on his face seemed more of an engagement in the discussion rather than putting Avni in discomfort by pressing more on the pressure that an interview brings.

"Anxiety, depression, and youth suicide are rising rapidly. People are relying on narcotics and guilty pleasures to escape reality instead of coping with it. As psychologists, our driving point is bringing humanity back amid civilization. Every human being has a true, genuine, authentic self. The trauma is the barrier, and healing is the only breakthrough."

"Why do you think such barriers occur?" Adi interrupted again. "Because it's too painful to be ourselves, because it's quite hard to face our demons. It is easier to point out mistakes or give solutions to others, but it becomes hard to stand for ourselves when the crisis happens. Suddenly, we feel powerless, helpless, and numb with our life, which can result in fear of facing one's own monsters," answered Avni.

"People are much lonelier and more isolated than they used to be. Solutions arise out of people when they confront themselves with the truth. I believe that people who are traumatized by medical ailments have a hard time expressing healthy anger."

"Yes, I agree, and that is what I am suffering with my wife now. I am trying to showcase her healthy anger." Said the doctor with a straight face.

"I am impressed, but let me tell you something, this isn't about knowing the theoretical part of it, but rather implementing it practically. It is hard work and can involve stressful, long hours, and in some cases, may damage your emotional health." Adi warned Avni about the job's responsibilities. "I promise I will not disappoint you," she answered confidently. "Then I would like to welcome my assistant right away," said the tall man with a sense of satisfaction.

She extended her thanks to the personality she idolized and left with her head held high.

"So Chetan, who wants to be perfect, must understand that this is life, not fiction." She woke up from her sleep with the sense of alertness that she might have found a way to heal Chetan.

❖

After specific experiences with patients, she understood that the standard template for all afflictions, mental illnesses, and physical diseases was trauma. When we realize that these traumatic responses and imprints are common and that we can work them through to become one authentic self, it is the way to deal with them.

Avni remembered Nalini, Adi's wife. She had hardly interacted with Nalini while she underwent treatment for her cancer. As Avni thought about Nalini now, she decided to stop by Nalini's home and spend quality time with her before starting work at the clinic.

Avni arrived at their place only to find many people present. Through bits and pieces of conversation, she realized, to her dismay, that Nalini had passed away. Avni felt sad and interacted with Adi with her condolences. "She fought hard against the cancer, but it overpowered her," Adi spoke with a low tone.

Adi requested Avni to take care of the clinic until he returned. "Take all the time you need." Avni left the place without uttering a word. She felt heavy, as if she had lost a great friend.

As Avni left, thoughts of Nalini filled her heart with warmth. She remembered Nalini's smile, her kindness, and how she always had time for a chat.

Avni arrived at the clinic and acknowledged the greetings from the receptionist. "Good morning. I'm filling in while Dr. Adi is away. How are the patients today?" Avni asked the receptionist.

"I heard the news. How is Adi coping?" The receptionist expressed condolences for Dr. Adi's loss. Avni responded respectfully but firmly, "Dr. Adi is taking his time grieving. Now, about the patients..."

The receptionist informed her, "I had to reschedule an appointment as you were late today."

Avni replied, "I apologize for the inconvenience. I forgot my keys to the cabin. May I please have the spare ones?"

"Sure, here is the duplicate key," the receptionist said, handing her a key chain with multiple keys.

Surprised, Avni asked, "You also have keys to the pharmacy?"

The receptionist matter-of-factly acknowledged this fact.

Avni responded firmly but politely, "For patient privacy and safety, I must request that pharmacy keys be restricted to authorized medical personnel only." The receptionist nodded in understanding.

Avni continued, "Please brief me on today's schedule to minimize further disruptions."

The receptionist provided the requested information in a compliant yet professional manner.

At her desk, Avni felt overwhelmed–Adi was on leave, Nalini had passed, and Chetan ignored her calls.

She dialed Chetan. Upon connecting, he revealed Vinay was dead. Her legs shook with fear–she had no idea of the turmoil within Chetan's family.

While she yearned to help Chetan with all her heart, his unresponsiveness frustrated her. She remembered Adi warned her not to push Chetan and to wait until the right moment. But Avni couldn't shake her sense of urgency.

She called Indira, Chetan's mother. Indira's distress sent adrenaline through Avni–some sinister threat to Chetan's family.

Avni rushed to meet Chetan in person. He was despondent, hollow-eyed from grief and lack of sleep. Avni fought back tears as she comforted him. She was convinced to give Chetan time to heal by himself. She wanted to take a few days off to be with Chetan, but unfortunately, Adi was on leave. So, in the absence of Adi, Avni had to take the main stage, and she got a call from the receptionist, who said that an appointment was scheduled in another 30 minutes. She reluctantly left the place.

A patient entered with eyes searching for Dr. Adi. Avni observed and said warmly, "Dr. Adi is away today, so I'm filling in. I'm sorry for the inconvenience." Avni added politely, "Would you like to reschedule for when Dr. Adi returns?"

The patient responded joyfully, "I'd like to share my excitement! This is all because of Dr. Adi." Avni learned the patient was an alcoholic receiving treatment for years.

"I am so happy. This is a dynamic that I never understood at first: confrontation with the truth will ensure that solutions arise. Now you can see how calm and content I am."

"I have lost an emotional attachment to my addiction, and now I can proudly say that when we lose an attachment to something, we realize how ordinary it was. My energy and attention made it so special," said the happy patient, who could not stop grinning.

The patient said gratefully, "I want to thank Dr. Adi and this clinic. I'm happy to say I've been off medications for 3 months now. I'm no longer addicted to alcohol and feel like I've dumped my trauma somewhere I can't get it back from. This is the first time in four years this has happened. I finally feel free."

Avni smiled widely. "That is such wonderful news! Your progress is a testament to your strength and resilience. You should be very proud of yourself. Somehow, you've gotten freer and younger. It gets better and better."

The patient beamed. "Dr. Adi's guidance helped me break free."

Avni reassured, "I'll pass along your gratitude when Dr. Adi returns. Keep up the good work!" The patient thanked Avni and left, spirits visibly lifted.

Though unable to meet Dr. Adi, the patient's joyful announcement filled Avni with warmth, reminding her of why they did this challenging work and the happiness that could result from overcoming their darkest struggles. So the energy of trauma could be transformed into the energy of life.

Experiences like these help remind us that every positive or negative situation is temporary and will eventually pass.

Trauma involves a lifelong pushing down of a tremendous expenditure of energy into not feeling the pain. As we heal, that same energy is liberated for life and for being in the present.

She took the patient's file and re-read the sessions he had

undergone. She wanted to find a quick and instant solution to Chetan's behavior.

The patient spoke, "I am addicted to alcohol. Too much that I left my family and kids. My parents abandoned me, which pushed me into loneliness, and I have abandoned my kids owing to my addiction. Please help me become a true, genuine, and authentic self. I want to come clean, I don't want to be guilty, and I don't want to be ashamed of myself."

"How did your parents abandon you?" questioned the doctor.

"Most people used to envy me for having a happy childhood. Coming from an upper-middle-class family, everything was given to me, but my parents were always too busy and used to shut me out of their way; that was their way of parenting."

"Slowly, when I moved into my adulthood, I got addicted to alcohol as I felt that it was my best companion to deal with my loneliness. And now, I feel I have inflicted the same trauma on my kids," said the man.

The doctor said that his behavior was a direct result of the trauma that he had experienced in his childhood. He continued, "When we talk about trauma, we usually think of something terrible happening to a person, but that's not the only trauma there is. The other kinds of trauma may not have to do with terrible things happening to you."

"So, when did you see yourself being deficient as a father and husband? Do you remember how your family felt?" The doctor continued the questioning.

"I just remember the pain of it instead of thinking why," cried the man.

"So what do you think your child has been into when his/her father is rude?" Questioned the doctor.

"It just hurts," said the man.

"It hurts because the man who is supposed to love them is being rude to them for actions they are not responsible for." The patient paused while he broke down.

"There are only two possibilities. Their father is a bad person who hates them, or they are bad people."

"So your kid's only protection is believing they are lovable. Who would you want your child to talk to in this circumstance?" The doctor continued with his interrogation.

"Myself," answered the man.

"Okay. When you used to have the same feeling, who did you talk to?" "No one."

"In other words, by the time you're five or six years old, you're completely alone. But I'm suggesting that your parents were traumatized. They must also have had adverse childhoods; they might have learned not to pay attention to their feelings, being the only way to survive."

"So they ignored you not because they didn't love you, but because they were shut down inside. It's multi-generational. You can't pick out who's at fault here. It didn't begin with anybody. It continues from one generation to the next," said the doctor.

"I felt ashamed," said the man.

"What have you done to subside the pain?" The doctor asked the patient.

"Alcohol. Self-hurt, however, the scrapes and bruises have faded now. My heart doesn't show any signs of subsiding from the guilt, regret, and pain." The patient responded.

"We have to give that consent to our hearts. Our bodies heal without permission, but not our hearts." The doctor responded.

This conversation, along with psychoanalysis sessions, had happened over four sessions, and now the addiction, pain, guilt, depression, everything had slowly disappeared from the man. Through the mist and the pain, he had learned to maintain, there was no shame.

Adi returned to work the next day. Avni chose not to share anything about what was happening in Chetan's family as he himself was grieving the loss of his wife, but she discussed with him the patients she had seen in his absence. "Are you okay? Do you want to take any time off work?" Adi asked upon seeing Avni's absent-minded reactions.

"I am okay," Avni responded. They continued with their usual business for the day.

THE DEADLOCK

After Vinay's funeral, Chetan sat vigil at his mother's side. The usually energetic house grew quiet, muffled in grief. His mother sat withdrawn in her sadness as Chetan wrestled with whether to question her about Lalit's mysterious death. His mother's lifeless behavior and red-rimmed eyes tore him, so he held his tongue, not wanting to cause more pain by questioning her this soon after Vinay's passing.

On the sixth day, Chetan reluctantly returned to work, leaving his mother alone in the large, empty house. As he went through the motions of his day, he could not help the anxiety flooding through him. Something about the two deaths nagged at him, the coincidences refusing to add up. He couldn't shake the feeling that his family had somehow become entangled in a drama far darker than he knew.

From Lalit's body, Chetan discovered a different perfume from Vinay's. However, Vinay's body had three different perfumes: one belonging to Vinay, another on his back, and a third with the syringe mark on his collar.

The autopsy revealed that Vinay died from a slow-acting poison that slowed his heart until it stopped. The blood around Vinay's body was not his, but they could not determine whose it was. Chetan requested forensics for DNA profiling. The crime scene and evidence suggested someone held Vinay from behind while another person injected the poison.

Chetan had clues but no solid leads. The multiple perfumes implied that at least three people were involved: Vinay and two others. The blood still remained a mystery.

Chetan struggled to navigate the investigation while supporting his grieving mother. Questioning her could provide valuable context, but might cause her more pain. Meanwhile, his intuition told him the deaths were linked, though the evidence remained circumstantial.

For now, Chetan focused on comforting his mother while quietly pursuing answers. He knew pushing her to reopen painful wounds could jeopardize any potential revelations she might someday choose to share. Patience and compassion, though difficult, might be the wiser path for now.

With bated breath, Chetan waited as his informants tailed the suspects who had purchased the soda bottles. One by one, they returned with descriptions of the suspects, until only one remained.

Suddenly, a breakthrough – the fingerprints recovered from Lalit's phone matched those of a man in the police database, a repeat nuisance offender arrested several times for petty crimes.

Chetan's heart raced as he saw the photo match the man who bought the soda bottle based on store surveillance footage and the description from the unresponsive informant. All the evidence pointed to this one stranger as a suspect.

This man was a complete enigma, seemingly unconnected to Lalit. Chetan urgently sent his photo for identification to Lalit's family, but no one recognized him. The gym manager remembered his face, recalling that he had tried to meet Lalit the day of the incident. The takeaway delivery person identified the man, saying he had seen him standing with Lalit for lunch that afternoon.

The pieces of the puzzle were falling rapidly into place,

rushing Chetan closer to the shocking truth about this mysterious stranger and his sinister connection to Lalit's death.

Chetan's instincts told him he had identified the man responsible for Lalit's murder. However, unlike his usual methodical process of building a case on concrete evidence, Chetan was acting hastily on a hunch.

Chetan's heart raced as he approached the suspect's residence. All the evidence pointed to this man, and Chetan was determined to bring him in.

As he rang the doorbell, an uneasy silence greeted him. No sound came from within the large home.

A chill ran down Chetan's spine. Something wasn't right. Bracing himself, he broke into the man's house.

The rooms were still and empty as Chetan made his way through, the unknown threatening to swallow him whole. He hastened towards the garden, desperate for any clue.

Then he smelled a foul, metallic odour that turned his stomach. Chetan's suspicions were confirmed as he came upon a gruesome discovery – the suspect's dead body, decaying in the garden.

The suspect was dead, but by whom? And why? The answers only seemed to lead to more questions as Chetan stared down at the corpse, the case suddenly taking a dark and twisted turn.

Chetan's shoulders slumped as the disappointing reality struck him. If this man had been Lalit's killer, then someone else had silenced him before Chetan could bring him to justice, further obscuring the truth. But if he was innocent, then an innocent man had been murdered, another mystery death added to Lalit's.

Either way, the killer remained free to kill again. Rather than being satisfied with catching Lalit's murderer, Chetan was overwhelmed by doubt. Finding the suspect already dead cast further uncertainty on Chetan's hastily formed theory that the man was Lalit's killer at all.

He had been so sure he was close to solving the case, but now all he had were more questions and another grieving family seeking answers.

As Chetan departed the crime scene, questions swirled in his head. His desire for answers had only uncovered more mysteries. He knew pursuing this case could endanger his life, but walking away might mean never finding justice for Lalit and Vinay. The choice weighed heavily on his heart.

Chetan's mind raced as he waited in line at the pharmacy, the stress and grief overwhelming him. Suddenly, he felt numbness in his hands and feet, and his heart started pounding. He leaned against the wall, breathing in panicked gasps as a cold sweat broke out. The store seemed to close around him, the voices and noises blurring into a dizzying mess.

After what felt like an eternity, the physical symptoms slowly eased, and he realized it was a panic attack. But the emotional anguish remained, weighing heavily on him.

His poor mother was already suffering so much that he could not burden her with his struggles. He would bear this pain alone, pushing through the exhaustion and despair one day at a time.

As he picked up his prescription with a forced smile for the pharmacist, Chetan's heart ached with the isolation of his suffering, wondering how much more grief his weary spirit could take before finally breaking.

He could not find any connection between Vinay and Lalit's murders or determine how the perpetrators committed the crimes. He received a call from forensics confirming that the DNA profiling matched 50% of his DNA sequence. "You inherit half of your DNA from each parent. This means about 50% of your DNA sequence will match one of your parents, and 50% will match the other parent. As we don't have your parents' samples, we can confirm the suspicion that the blood sample is from one of your parents." Chetan was stumped upon hearing this. He had lost his father earlier in his childhood, and the only one left on this planet was his mother.

Chetan turned the case over and over in his mind, a niggling suspicion growing that wouldn't let him rest. Something was not adding up.

All the clues eventually led back to that final phone call Lalit made to Chetan's mother just before his death–a phone call she claimed to know nothing about.

Chetan's jaw clenched as he remembered his mother's evasive answers whenever he'd brought up the case. Her odd defensiveness and eagerness for him to move on. His heart sank at the dark thought in his mind, but he couldn't dismiss it.

As he gazed at his grieving mother now, her innocence once unquestionable now clouded with doubt, Chetan steeled himself to get the answers he needed. The case had never truly been solved, and the bitter suspicion was growing that the culprit might have been hiding in plain sight all along.

He stepped into the house, an ominous stillness filling the air. He built up his courage and visited his mother's bedroom around nine that evening. Chetan's emotional heart clashed with his overactive mind, making things worse.

He found his mother's lifeless form, unmoving and pulseless, lying back in her chair. Shock crashed over him in cold, horrific waves as the terrible truth struck him–she had silently slipped away. With numb fingers, he mechanically called for an ambulance, though in his heart, he knew that she was gone. Darkness crowded his vision as he gazed upon the tragic scene, unable to comprehend the enormity of the grief within him.

As he gathered her still form into his arms, rocking and weeping, the cold silence of the house was shattered by Chetan's anguished cries of loss and heartbreak for the woman who had been his whole world.

Chetan collapsed at her side, a sob tearing from his lips. He clutched her hand, now cold as stone, and covered it with kisses. "My dearest mother," he whispered through tears. "How will I go on without you?"

The discovery of his mother's body pushed Chetan to the brink of despair. Not only had he lost his chance at answers about Vinay and Lalit's murders, but he had also lost the woman who gave him life. His blind obsession with justice had caused him to miss other threats right under his nose.

As the paramedics confirmed his mother's passing, Chetan collapsed in anguish. In his single-minded pursuit to uncover his brother's killer, he failed to protect the one family member he had left–his mother.

Chetan was struck by the realization that you never know when your last hug, eye contact, or goodbye with a person would be. He reminisced about the day the three had dinner together. He had been hopeful his mother could help with Vinay and Lalit's case, but never imagined he would have to investigate her death as well.

Chetan sat there for hours, head on his mother's chest, weeping openly for his loss. Avni accompanied him in his grief. Thoughts of vengeance fled his mind, replaced by an aching void where his beloved mother once stood. All he had now were memories and the silent house where he would never again hear her voice.

Grief consumed Chetan as he wondered if he would ever learn the truth. His mother's death suggested a deeper conspiracy at play, one that even she remained unable to escape. The killer remained one step ahead, adept at covering his tracks. His mind never stopped asking himself how his mother's blood was at the crime scene where Vinay was murdered.

Chetan knew he must push through his despair to honor his family. His mother's passing had complicated the case further.

THE LAST HOPE

Weeks passed in a blur. Avni arrived at Chetan's flat, her heart dropping as she saw his state. He sat motionless in the dim room, staring blankly ahead. When Avni called his name, he did not respond.

Tears sprang to Avni's eyes as she rushed to Chetan, holding him tightly. "My dear, what happened?" She sobbed.

Chetan numbly recounted finding his mother lifeless, just like his brother before her. He had been miserable for days, waiting for death to claim him, too. It seemed like a dark curse had swept through their lives.

Avni's heart broke for his unimaginable loss and pain. She sat beside him, letting him weep on her shoulder. "You are not alone," she said gently, stroking his hair. "I am here for you."

She listened patiently as he reminisced about memories with his mother and brother, their smiles and laughter, now only ghosts of the past. She cooked meals for him and stayed by his side through the long nights as sobs wracked his weary frame.

While Chetan's grief would never completely leave him, Avni's unwavering companionship helped him find the strength to keep living, honoring his family's memories with each passing minute. Finding a positive response, Avni suggested that Chetan visit Adi so that he could gain emotional strength to find the culprits.

Chetan realized his emotional state clouded his thinking and was impeding the investigation. He knew he needed to manage his grief healthily to think clearly. Though the journey would be long, with help, he could regain mental clarity to honor his loved ones and pursue justice, one step at a time.

Though reluctant to share his struggles, Chetan agreed to accept Avni's support.

The next day, Chetan met Dr. Adi. After Avni introduced them, Chetan sat down. Adi noticed that Chetan looked physically and emotionally drained.

Avni expressed her concern for Chetan's well-being. Chetan appreciated their care and realized opening up would be difficult but necessary.

Dr. Adi spoke gently, "How are you doing, young man? I've heard great things about your deductive skills. What brings you here today?"

Chetan shared, "I've been experiencing intense fear, sadness, anger, guilt, and helplessness lately. These emotions have become overwhelming and difficult to manage."

Adi said, "It's okay to ask for help. Taking that first step shows you care for yourself, as you've done today. Trust me with your struggles–whatever you're comfortable sharing."

Adi asked, "Are you able to focus on your work?"

Chetan replied, "I've been having trouble concentrating at work lately. Unwanted thoughts and memories keep popping into my head. I have headaches, tension, fatigue, and trouble sleeping."

Adi gently asked, "What's been on your mind?"

Chetan described the recent gruesome incidents and the panic attacks he had been having lately. Avni comforted him.

Adi responded compassionately, "I'm sorry for your loss and struggles. It takes courage to share such painful experiences. Your mind and feelings are both important. Feelings fuel actions, but it's the mind that provides clarity."

"I can't stop asking myself why I hate myself so much that I suddenly decided that life is unbearable. How do I soothe myself when there is no peace inside?" Chetan pleaded with the doctor.

Adi reassured Chetan, "Your feelings are valid, but won't hold you back forever. Remember who you are at your core."

Chetan described growing up in a nurturing family, which fueled his ambition.

Adi asked, "What matters most to you moving forward?"

Chetan realized he wanted to honor his family's values of truth and justice.

Adi promised, "I'll help you manage your emotions healthily."

"Instead of focusing on panic attacks, let's start by talking through a stressful memory in a way that gives you closure. I would like you to describe situations where you have had panic attacks."

Chetan described the same to Adi.

Adi asked if there were only three situations where he had had them. "Looks like you are having the attacks before going towards a dead body. Can you please tell me about a recent episode when you were upset?"

The doctors stayed silent to give Chetan a moment to gather courage to continue.

"Can you please explain the trigger points?" The doctor asked the patient, referring to an attack.

"Of late, my mind has not been stronger than my feelings. I was so motivated by my mother's words that I continued my work. At one point, I felt like it was too much of an ask for my brain to process those traumatic reasons for my clients' deaths. As I prepared to quit, my mother pushed me to work harder for society. I picked up Lalit's case," Chetan described Lalit's case history and the subsequent incidents involving his brother and mother.

Both Avni and Adi felt bad for Chetan's state. Avni held his hand through the rest of the story.

"Do you know who did that?" Avni questioned Chetan.

Chetan shook his head no. "You cannot rush when your emotions overpower the mind. Your mind has to be stronger than your feelings. I cannot zero in on the suspects with the current state of my mind."

"I have lost the one I believed to be the answer to my every question," Chetan remembered his mother.

"I agree your feelings keep you in bed whereas your mind asks you to get up," said the doctor, empathizing with Chetan.

"What is your fear of being about?" The doctor questioned the detective.

"That I am not trying hard enough to bring justice to the people, and I am afraid of accepting the truth that my family is no more," Chetan answered.

"Tell me more about yourself and why you feel so." The doctor took it as an opportunity to understand the patient.

"I was the eldest of two, a very ambitious family, very successful, except we were raised by my mother all by herself."

"What about your father?" The doctor interrupted and extended his apologies upfront, if it was a sensitive topic. "He passed away when I was a toddler."

"I am sorry to hear that. How did it happen?"

"He committed suicide as he failed to battle through depression," Chetan conveyed.

Trying to redirect the conversation positively, Adi asked, "What qualities did you inherit from your parents that have served you well?"

Chetan thought momentarily and said, "My mother's resilience and determination. She raised us on her own through hard work and sacrifice."

The doctor smiled and said, "Those are wonderful strengths that will continue to help guide you through difficult times."

"How was your childhood?" Adi added.

"Ours is the most affluent family in town. I have taken the path of a criminologist, whereas my mother and brother have taken care of our business." Chetan told about his family bond.

"What is it that keeps you awake when you are battling the suffering of your family members' demise?" Adi, with a soft tone.

"The questions keep me awake–what link did my mother have with Lalit, and how come my brother got inside an abandoned house?" Chetan responded.

"So it's a good thing that your diversion from trauma is your addiction towards work," Adi lauded Chetan's efforts.

THE KNOTS

Chetan continued with the case, which had now come to a halt with Lalit's suspected killer dead. Chetan was at a loss, with nothing to move forward with. On the other hand, Avni and Adi keenly paid attention to Chetan's healing journey.

Chetan desperately needed answers about his brother's death. He pored over the blood droplets he collected from the crime scene, searching for any clue that might have been missed.

Unable to think clearly through his emotions, he recruited a team of investigators to help. They combed the scene meticulously for any evidence, but the murder appeared well-planned, with the killer leaving no trace behind.

Frustration began to settle in as dead ends emerged. He wanted nothing more than to find the person responsible for his brother's murder.

Chetan desperately needed a breakthrough as the case started to seem hopeless due to a lack of leads. So, he sent soil samples from the abandoned room to university analysts.

Small rocks and bits were consistent with material stuck to a suspect's shoes (confirmed from the shoe traces). Geologists and mineralogists pored over the samples.

They found tiny glass fragments, likely from bottles, and copper ash that could only have been produced by a copper smelter. But samples from Lalit's location and the dead suspect's body lacked such copper ash, indicating only the crime scene soil where Vinay had been killed contained both glass and copper ash.

The geologist determined that a nearby copper smelting plant, hundreds of meters from the crime scene, was the only source of copper ash in the area.

Chetan's pulse quickened as he verified with the constable, who identified his brother's body–the constable didn't live anywhere near that copper plant. A thrill of realization rushed through him–the crime scene soil pointed to a different suspect, one linked to the copper smelter. After so many dead ends, the team finally had a solid lead pointing towards the real killer.

There were a few possibilities for the potential suspect's connection to the copper smelting plant:

1. The suspect worked at the plant, either as an employee or a contractor. This would explain why soil from the plant was found on their shoes and clothing. Workers at the plant would pass through the gate in the surveillance footage regularly.

2. The suspect lived near the plant, perhaps in employee housing or a neighboring area. This proximity would result in regular exposure to the soil and ash from the plant, tracking it to other locations. In this case, the suspect's frequent passing through the plant gate would be unsurprising.

3. The suspect was a regular visitor but had no formal connection to the plant. They might go there to meet someone, dispose of items, engage in illegal activities, or for other purposes.

4. It's possible the suspect had no actual connection to the plant at all and was only there once on the day of the murder to dispose of evidence.

In summary, the soil evidence and surveillance footage strongly pointed to the suspect having a legitimate, routine connection to the copper smelting plant as an employee, neighbour, or regular visitor. However, the limited information made it difficult to determine the exact nature of the relationship.

The breakthrough with soil evidence gave hope. They obtained surveillance footage from the copper plant's gates, focusing on people passing on foot during the time of death to match the evidence.

The team scanned the footage frame by frame, creating a list of suspects based on time and appearance. An excited energy filled the room as they finally zeroed in on potential leads.

The team hit the streets, actively investigating each suspect. All checks came back negative–except for one.

When they tried contacting the suspect's neighbors and friends, no one knew his whereabouts. People in the neighborhood confirmed no activity near the suspect's house for days.

A thrill of anticipation shot through Chetan as he realized they might have finally found the man. The suspect's sudden disappearance right after the murder, combined with the soil evidence linking him to the copper plant, was too much to be a coincidence.

After a painstaking search, the crucial pieces of the puzzle were finally falling into place. Chetan could barely contain his excitement as he briefed his team. Justice for Vinay now seemed within their grasp.

His heart pounded as they approached the suspect's home. No one answered the doorbell, so they forcefully entered the room. While there were no apparent signs of foul play, Chetan detected the faint smell of muriatic acid, often used to cover blood stains; he had spotted a perfume bottle matching the scent found on Vinay's body–concrete evidence built against the person, proving him to be the real killer.

As they continued their search, a gruesome discovery was made–a man's body stuffed in a cupboard, preserved with chemicals to prevent odor.

His pulse quickened as he realized this cast doubts on

whether the killer was a professional. He left the place in distress.

A thorough examination of every clue–soil samples, footage, and chemical evidence- pointed them towards another body. This made him feel even more demotivated and hopeless. His need to bring justice to his brother had become nothing but a line drawn in water.

They had sent the body for forensic analysis and understood that the chemicals used mainly were common food preservatives.

Chetan fell at once with a sudden onset of intense fear. His breathing became rapid and shallow. He felt tingly and numb all over and thought he might be experiencing a heart attack. For the first time in his life, he dialed up an ambulance for himself. The episode subsided within 30 minutes, and the doctors diagnosed it as a panic attack.

Meanwhile, one of the team members had come up with a list of centers that held the poison. The poison injected into Vinay's body had been available across many hospitals, and it was not a cakewalk to identify a single center.

❖

"When Avni used to praise your deduction skills and work for the department, I used to think she exaggerated. But now, I must say that I am impressed with your skills, though your emotional state is unstable, the focus on your work is merely affected." The doctor said to the detective.

The detective acknowledged the thoughtful critique with a subtle nod. Though the compliment warmed him, the doctor's mention of his instability struck a nerve. The case involving those murders had consumed and agonized him for weeks.

"Although I used to be unmoved by any praise and didn't believe in the concept of psychiatry, I feel rekindled after you acknowledge my skill amid emotional pain. Maybe this is what a psychiatrist's magic is," Chetan responded.

The doctor continued, "Your thorough examination of the evidence, considering all possibilities without premature conclusions, reveals a finely honed mind. Yet you cannot let your emotional investment blind you. You must stay methodical."

"Unfortunately, the rage in my mind is discomforting," Chetan said about his situation.

"This could be the reason for your syndrome. Do not seek revenge. Revenge and rage blind you emotionally, leading to panic attacks. Leave the perpetrator to justice. That is the only way to honor these deaths. When I listen to you, I understand that you have started getting panic attacks only when the memories and feelings attached to the ones you are emotionally bound to are involved."

Chetan acknowledged that the doctor was right; he had to regain discipline, shed emotion, and pursue the truth with clear eyes.

The doctor suggested using relaxation techniques and practicing regularly, including deep breathing, progressive muscle relaxation, visualization, and guided imagery, which can help short-circuit a panic attack and relieve anxiety between episodes.

Chetan shared his struggles openly, "Guided imagery has made my situation worse. When I close my eyes to focus on something positive, images of my loved ones' deaths flood my mind, racing my heart."

The therapist listened compassionately. "Facing such painful memories can feel overwhelming. But avoiding them won't help either."

"Have you gotten any more anxiety attacks after that?" Avni asked her man.

"Yes, after I followed the leads I had captured at the incident where the man was stuffed inside his cupboard," Chetan continued.

"What are they?" Both doctors questioned him at once.

An awkward silence set in the room, as the doctors understood they were showing more enthusiasm towards the leads than focusing on Chetan.

Chetan shared with the doctors in a calm but somber tone. The doctors listened closely, seeing past his pale expression to the strength within.

"The pieces of the puzzle were slowly coming together. Clues pointed to several possibilities: kitchen preservatives, muriatic acid, and matching fibers found on both victims' bodies."

"My pulse quickened as we discovered strands of identical fibers on both corpses. Suddenly, a chilling realization struck me–the deaths of Lalit, Vinay, and my mother seemed related, though different from the other trailing murders."

"We have categorized the murders: Lalit, Vinay, and my mother's deaths are linked as they knew each other. The other category included the random murders: one body found in a backyard, the other stuffed in a cupboard, concealed with the same evidence."

"My only hope was the insects feeding on the bodies–they could be the only leads to solve that gruesome puzzle. As the forensics team examined the insects for clues, I held my breath, feeling we were finally closing in on the twisted mind behind the meticulously planned but messy executions."

"Though the victims lived far apart, the autopsies revealed the random murders happened within hours of each other, strengthening my theory that a single killer was responsible for those two deaths. The additional evidence collected from the crime scene was a shank button found in the deceased's fist, coated with food preservatives."

"How did the deceased get the shank button in his fist? The shank button didn't match any shirts at the victim's place. Adding to the possibility that the victim must have gotten it while fighting with the killer. Items were scattered, indicating a struggle. Evidence included fibers, buttons, and preservatives pointing to a possible suspect."

"But the question remained: how did the killer manage to commit the murders in such a short amount of time, despite the significant distance between the crime scenes? Clearly, the killer was familiar with the area and knew a shortcut known to only a few. The killer must have killed the first one and later moved on to the second in under 30 minutes. The main route will take at least 90 minutes to reach victim 2."

"The killer had left behind a trail of clues, but nothing seemed to add up. We collected samples of DNA evidence, including blood, but none matched any known criminals. The fingerprints and blood samples found at the crime scenes didn't lead us to any suspects either. There were no eyewitnesses to speak about the heinous crime that could give more clues."

"Adding to the mystery was the fact that the victims had no apparent link to each other or to the other three people who were also murdered in the area. The motive for the murders remained unclear, and we were left with more questions than answers."

"How should I proceed further? Had the evidence been re-analyzed by a different lab? I did so that a fresh set of eyes on the DNA, fibers, etc., could uncover something previously missed. Nothing helped further."

"I spent hours and hours developing a suspect profile. I had put up evidence and links between both the victims and created a profile of what type of person might have committed these crimes. Looking for potential suspects who fit that mold, the shank button was what I was after."

"I had traced the steps of each victim before their death. Reconstructed their activities, connections, and whereabouts in the days and hours before being killed. That did expose a possible link between them, but it was too fast to conclude."

"What was the link?" Avni interrupted Chetan. Adi was eager too.

"It was very vague," answered Chetan.

"Please continue," they both forgot they were after a patient who needed their help. Avni stopped taking notes.

Chetan continued excitedly, "The acid and preservatives used to clean the floor and body were a major lead. Forensics confirmed that large food chains often use this preservative to preserve food, so it had to be bought in bulk, not from a normal store. So our search area was shortened. It suggested either big food stores that had had them for a long time or big wholesale markets that sell the preservatives."

"I searched every possible lead by combing through all the supermarkets that sold the preservatives and frequently purchasing customers of that brand from the stores. Fortunately, we found a match with a restaurant that matched the description–the restaurant cafeteria we often visit!" Chetan told Avni.

Avni's heart began pounding. Their favorite restaurant–a place they considered so safe and familiar–could somehow be connected to these gruesome murders.

The case finally took a terrifying twist, revealing that even the safest places can hide the darkest secrets.

Avni asked Chetan who the killer was. His gaze towards Avni turned into anger. Avni was terrified and confused.

Chetan hurriedly recounted how the restaurant bought those particular preservatives in bulk. He continued his story with rising excitement, "Once I was in the restaurant, I observed that the waiter/partner we knew well wasn't there and found out that he was away from work for quite a long time."

"All the clues pointed to him: the preservatives missing from the kitchen matched those on the victim's body; the muriatic acid rack was empty, and the formula matched what was used on the floor; the shirt button was his–I remembered the unique buttons from when we met to discuss cracking an interview with Adi, the shirt he wore in his latest post had that same unique button; the fibers and foam padding shreds came from his car–he used foam padding for treating his sit bones; I remember his social media feed where he posted daily about body transformations, but he hasn't posted for quite some time–the same time frame as the murders."

Avni's heart raced as the evidence stacked up against their waiter partner. He had seemed so harmless, yet was now the prime suspect for the gruesome killings.

Chetan spoke with rising intensity, "All the clues point to him, but we have no proof. We must gather more evidence to build an airtight case against him!"

Avni nodded, exhilarated yet fearful. They had to catch this twisted killer before he struck again, even if confronting him meant walking into danger. Justice for the victims demanded nothing less.

Avni could barely contain her shock.

"Did you find him? Why did he stop posting?" Avni implored Chetan, while Adi listened intently.

"I had a gut feeling something bad happened to him," Chetan said grimly.

"What bad?" Adi interrupted.

"His neighbors said he'd left for his hometown a few days ago. I made my way there and found out he had committed suicide by consuming poison. His funeral had already taken place by the time I reached." Chetan's hands trembled.

An ominous silence fell over the room, a tense, suffocating atmosphere.

"You had a panic attack then?" The doctor asked, breaking the silence.

"Yes," the man replied, explaining the type of panic attack

he'd experienced.

"I was so close to catching the killer," Chetan said darkly. "But instead, he took the coward's way out. Now we may never know the truth behind those gruesome murders, or why he felt the need to take his own life."

The doctors listened attentively as the man recounted his story, pain evident in his voice. Through his words, they could visualize the events that had occurred.

THE CIRCLING OF THE KNOTS

"So, how was the waiter linked to all the cases?" Avni asked impatiently.

"From our investigation, we concluded the waiter had hired strangers to kill Lalit and Vinay initially," he explained. "Then he killed them both himself, as the evidence all pointed back to him."

"However, what's puzzling is why he chose to poison my mother and brother, giving them a relatively painless death, while brutally murdering the others." Chetan's voice wavered. "Did he not want to cause my family suffering, even in death?"

"Your mother died of poison?" Avni asked tentatively.

"Yes, the same poison he used to kill my brother and himself," Chetan replied grimly.

Avni fired off more questions, and the mystery only deepened. "What was his motive? Where did he find the people who killed Lalit and Vinay? How did he convince them to commit murder? Why didn't you identify them in your records if they were criminals? If not, how did he even know them?"

Chetan ran his hands through his hair in frustration. "I don't have the answers yet. This waiter somehow had connections with ruthless killers and even hired strangers to commit murders. But I still don't understand his motive for involving my family at all, much less sparing my mother and brother with pain in their deaths."

Adi's pulse quickened as a chilling realization struck him. "Chetan, what if he knew your family personally? What if he had a twisted motive for specifically sparing them pain?"

Chetan paled. "You think... he could have been targeting me all along? Using the others as a cover to get away with killing my mother and brother?"

"Have you been targeted?" Adi asked anxiously. "Didn't you cross paths with any of the victims?"

"That's a critical question," Chetan replied. "The two victims the waiter managed to convince were emotionally unstable, like me. Not me, but you had certainly crossed your path with them. One battled a gambling addiction and the other an alcohol addiction. They both had visited your clinic for treatment in the past few months."

Both Avni and Adi were stuck in dire shock. "What do you mean by this?" Avni raised her voice as her legs trembled with fear.

Adi's eyes widened. "So, the waiter was specifically targeting vulnerable people."

Chetan nodded grimly. "It seems he preyed on those he perceived as weak-willed and easy to manipulate. But I still don't know why he needed to involve my family."

Adi frowned. "It seems personal if he poisoned your mother and brother while brutally murdering the others."

"Let's hear from our beloved Avni," Chetan said ominously. "Were you not the last one to speak with them?" Chetan questioned Avni, his tone accusatory.

Stunned, Avni replied, "How can you conclude that?" She couldn't believe Chetan would confront her. He was suspecting her. It felt like her worst nightmare came true. Her heart began racing.

Chetan's eyes bored into hers as he spoke. "The evidences

point to you. The fibers, the poisons, the victims' last calls all trace back to you!"

Avni struggled to breathe, tears welling up as she protested. "I would never hurt anyone! You have to believe me!"

But Chetan seemed unconvinced. Avni's world came crashing down around her. The possibility that her own loved one could think her capable of such horrors cut deep into her soul.

"Please," she begged Chetan, her voice breaking. "You know I could never commit these crimes." She looked at him desperately, hoping he would see the truth in her eyes.

Adi raised his voice, pointing to Chetan, "How can you accuse Avni without proper evidence?"

He continued, "You cannot make such serious accusations against someone based only on circumstantial evidence and suspicion. Have you considered that there may be reasonable explanations for your presented facts?"

Chetan continued, "Yes, I have managed it through victim profiling. I have six victims–some related, some not. If it were one family, why wasn't I targeted? Lalit, my mother's accountant, was killed. Were there financial obligations involved in any of her businesses? Is it something linked to the same business that bothered my mother when I visited her? How did a gambler and alcoholic become involved? Did they know each other?"

"The fact that I was not targeted, despite being related to two of the victims, indicates the killer's motives may be more personal and focused on select individuals rather than the whole family. This points to someone who knew the victims personally."

Avni trembled with fear. She couldn't believe what was happening. Neither could Adi.

"When was the last time you spoke with my mother? My brother? The waiter? The gambling addict? The alcohol addict?"

Chetan questioned Avni, but she stayed numb.

Chetan explained, "The answers lie in tracing the victims' activities in the last 6 months. All 6 have two things in common."

The doctor adjusted his voice and asked, "What are they?"

"A vehicle was seen at the crime scene on the days of the crimes. At first, I thought it was a coincidence, as the same vehicle was observed a day before or after the crime, but not at or during the time of the crime. However, it was not. So, who does that vehicle belong to? And the poison used on Vinay, my mother, and the waiter is available here at your very own clinic. Who controls it?"

Silence filled the room. Chetan's logical analysis and questions left Avni and Adi speechless and fearful. The prevalence of the exact vehicle at multiple crime scenes and the presence of the same poison used in at least three killings indicate these were not random, disconnected crimes. They were likely perpetrated by the same culprit using accessible means.

Chetan calmly yet firmly pursued the truth, piecing together clues pointing to someone close within that clinic. The killer's access to the poison in the clinic likely meant he worked there or had close connections with someone who did. This pointed the finger of suspicion against Avni, Adi, and other clinic employees/associates. Chetan told his intention towards the receptionist.

Avni recollected that the receptionist had the key to the pharmacy that contained the poison. She looked at the reception through the glass doors, but the receptionist was unavailable at the desk.

"But how could Avni, who has shown me so much love and compassion, be behind all this?" Chetan said, pain evident in his voice.

"I've had more panic attacks than usual during this difficult investigation. My emotions ran so high that I began to suspect even those closest to me."

Adi spoke firmly but kindly, "If you truly believe Avni is innocent, as you claim, then you must give her the benefit of the doubt. You know her heart and character; does anything about her suggest she could be capable of such horrible crimes?"

"I have examined all the evidence meticulously," Chetan began. "Something kept bothering me about these crimes. They involved victims from different walks of life, yet it happened with such precision and planning as if they knew everything about the victims. Does Avni have this much capability?"

He paused, letting the implications hang in the air as the doctor anxiously sipped his coffee. Chetan continued. "A vehicle was spotted at each crime scene–before and after. At first, I dismissed it, but then I traced each victim's movements. Their paths all converged at one place: this clinic."

The doctor trembled with fear as he softly asked, "Whose vehicle was it?"

Chetan responded firmly but calmly, meeting the doctor's uneasy gaze. "The same vehicle I saw in the magazine when Avni showed your profile."

The doctor started to shake, spilling coffee onto the table. Chetan stood firm. The doctor began to protest, but Chetan silenced him with a steely glance.

"Then there is the poison." Chetan's voice remained steady. "Accessible only to those within these walls. Used to end lives...and cover tracks."

"The vehicle. The poison." Chetan's tone softened slightly. "Only one person had the means, motive, and opportunity for all these deaths. The question remains: why?"

Silence filled the room for some time, and the doctor broke down, his trembling apologies slipping from his lips. As Chetan listened, horror and grief washed over him. But justice was finally within reach.

Avni gasped in shock and horror. Adi, the kind doctor who had helped so many, was behind these monstrous killings? It couldn't be true.

But Chetan's calm yet cutting questions and deductions left no room for doubt. Avni felt sick, her legs trembling. "You have mastered remaining calm," Adi praised Chetan.

"Still, the question remains the same: why?" Chetan stood firmly.

The doctor pleaded with Chetan. "Don't you know the motive when you know all this?"

Avni finally found her voice, "But Adi, why? How could you?"

Chetan sighed wearily. "Motive can be elusive. Revenge, madness, delusion...these things cloak themselves in warped justifications. However, you missed one thing in this entire act."

Both the doctor and Avni looked at Chetan. "A silly mistake that criminals usually commit. Not researching the solid facts."

Chetan took a deep breath, steeling himself for what must be said.

"At first, I thought the actions and killings were part of the usual plan," he began. "But later I realized I had misunderstood. You made a mistake."

"Vinay is not your biological son," he said gently but firmly. "The truth is... I am."

Shock spread across Adi's face, followed by sorrow and regret. For years, he had wondered about the son who didn't share his dark complexion or features. Now, the reality had come crashing down.

He trembled. "How... how did you find out? It cannot be true."

Chetan's gaze was soft but weary. "I found the will, documents...hints of a truth you've kept hidden all these years."

"What will? What son? He doesn't have kids, right? Your

father died by suicide when you were a toddler, right? Can you help me here?" Avni continued her questions to calm her racing heart.

Tears filled Chetan's eyes. He spilled the facts, "I was adopted by my mother from Mr. and Mrs. Adi, who are my biological parents, and Indira, my foster mother. My foster father died just before I was adopted."

Avni remembered the story Adi had told Dhwani, the woman who had an abortion, that the adoption was real.

"You should have killed me," Chetan said. "I deserved not to live on this planet after taking birth from such a monstrous father."

Silence filled the air with the weight of years lost to half-truths and omissions.

Then Chetan said, "While the past cannot change, the future is unwritten. Vinay was still my brother in every way that mattered. And Indira will still be my mother, the woman who raised me and loved me the best she could."

The doctor buried his head in his hands. When he spoke, his voice cracked with sorrow. "I only wanted to help. The addictions, the suffering. I tried everything." Adi tried to gain sympathy by showcasing that the deaths are without any strong motive, and was trying to calm down the emotional agony.

"But you cannot use it for your motive," Chetan spoke with a strong voice.

"How could you do all these?" Avni could not believe that she worked for a murderer.

"You think killing is hard after you see how hard it is to heal someone? You can break anything in seconds, but it takes forever to fix it. I have fixed myself by opting for those killings," Adi spoke with no regret and as confidently as ever. "You still don't feel regret even after seeing your biological son before you?" Chetan questioned him.

"Why should I, when I had already made peace with it years ago? It all started thirty years ago. Nalini and I were leading a happy life as a young couple in London. We discovered that we were pregnant with a baby boy. As young parents-to-be in London, Nalini dreamed of raising our child together."

He paused. "The realities of parenthood were daunting. I was not ready for the responsibilities of fatherhood. My career demanded focus at that stage. I was not ready to be separated, although Nalini forced me to do so as I depended on her for my educational finances."

Chetan interjected, "Were you married then?"

"No," he said smugly. "That helped me convince Nalini to give up the child. She was initially reluctant, but I leveraged her insecurities and fears of facing the challenges alone at such a young age."

He continued proudly, "I convinced her it was for the best and that we could continue our lives as if nothing had happened. She agreed, and I cut all ties, continuing my career unburdened."

His voice hardened, "So you see, I have no regrets. I did what I had to do. The past is the past."

Chetan saw the calculating gleam in the man's eyes, the lack of remorse. It was clear he felt no guilt for the pain he had caused. His actions had been driven purely by self-interest and expediency.

The man's voice was heavy but not regretful. "Though it broke Nalini's heart, we sought out an adoption agency and found Indira for him. As far as I knew then, Indira didn't have kids, and you were her first. She told us about her husband's sudden demise and the reason for adopting a kid at that age. She was young and a successful entrepreneur."

After welcoming you, Indira made a pact with us. She didn't want the child ever to know the truth, so she asked us not to make any contact after signing the papers. I agreed and gave the child away without hesitation. The pact also stated that we would never reveal the truth ourselves and that no part of our property would be passed on to the child.

We were back from London. To honor the promise made to Indira, Nalini wanted us to be downtown and not leave the place until we received a call from Indira. The pledge to Nalini bound me, as she had the complete right to our property. My life as a successful physician had been spent downtown with fewer patients and less fame. I worked hard to earn my name across cities and countries. We spoke briefly about the adoption incident afterwards, and seldom talked about moving up to the town to honor our careers.

Time passed, and cancer took Nalini most cruelly. With limited resources downtown, we moved here, and I opened my clinic. The years of longing for the child she'd given away weighed heavily on Nalini. She was always mad, and it had become impossible to calm her down. I reluctantly agreed with her to meet Indira.

Nalini was overjoyed with the decision. She contacted Indira and told her about the situation. Indira visited us along with Vinay, whom Nalini saw for the first time in years. Vinay stayed out of the room, and Indira entered where my wife was being treated. Looking at her after a long time made me feel vicious. I was once happy to see her, as she took away my burden, but not anymore.

Avni looked at the doctor in dismay and said, "But you work in charity and have no issue giving wealth to those in need. I cannot believe what you're implying."

The doctor replied gently, "It's not really about the money. It's making peace with the fact that I have to give up something I once viewed as mine, to someone I once saw as an obstacle. That thought weighs heavily on the healing mind."

"How did you think Vinay was your biological son?" Chetan

asked the doctor to continue his story.

Nalini asked Indira about the person standing outside the room, to which Indira replied that it was her son. We assumed Vinay was the child she'd adopted. Nalini spoke to Indira, asking her to honor her final wish–to pass the assets to Vinay after her death. Though Indira initially refused, Nalini was unwilling to accept her denial. Reluctantly, Indira agreed, moved by the weight of Nalini's last request.

"I could not stay calm, knowing that all the assets I have owned go to someone who doesn't even know they exist. I could not let this happen."

"I visited your mom's house and asked her not to sign the documents Nalini sent her. She disagreed. I spoke with Lalit, your mother's accountant, when he visited me for the proceedings, and he threatened me with legal obligations. I thought of asking Vinay to be on my side, and after knowing the truth, he denied it to my face, which forced me to inject the poison into him."

"Why did you use innocent people?" Chetan questioned.

The doctor responded, "I did not want to risk losing my freedom by getting caught handling the situation myself."

Chetan countered, "But by manipulating others into committing murders on your behalf, you violated your ethics and their freedom."

Horror dawned on Avni and Chetan as the truth emerged in all its monstrous clarity. The doctor, blinded by righteousness, had felt called to end what he saw as hopeless lives. "They did not have any purpose; however, they felt emotionally detached from their sufferings only after killing the people," the doctor supported his intentions.

"How did you manage to convince them?" Chetan questioned his monstrous father.

"I used the drug that expands the consciousness among the patients. The first target–the alcoholic who had the rage of his parents, avoiding him as they were busy with their lives. I directed him to Lalit, who was a busy accountant."

"The second target–the gambler who had raged upon his friend who forced him into gambling. I directed him to Vinay. However, he was not able to finish his work, and I had to enter the scene and inject the poison," Adi spoke of the actual happenings of the incidents. "That's how I injured myself," he showed his right palm at the right longitudinal crease between his thumb and index finger.

Chetan recalled the blood droplet with 50% DNA evidence of his at Vinay's crime scene.

"How did the waiter come into the picture, as he hasn't met you?" Avni questioned, as she knew the waiter was a fan of Adi's work, but had never met him.

Adi responded, saying that the waiter had met him to discuss the trauma he had when Avni was away.

"What was that?" Avni asked the question.

"He had accumulated anger towards people who disrespected him. Every time he met a person, there was a tinge of anger when he realized that the person was not listening to or being attentive to him. So all I had to do was direct him towards both addicts. He did the work, but unfortunately, he failed to dispose of the bodies without eliminating the evidence." As Adi spoke, Avni showed her disgust.

"When did you replace my mother's eye drops?" Chetan resisted pointing out the weapon used on his mother.

"I had observed that Indira was using eye drops to treat her dry eyes. I replaced that with a bottle filled with poison when I visited her for the second time while handing over the documents. She killed herself," the doctor cleaned his plate by saying that she had done it to herself.

Avni spoke now, her voice gentle yet pained. "I cannot imagine you knew all this and yet sat calmly confronting the truth with the criminal?" She held Chetan, who was controlling himself, while the tears rolled down his face.

"You cannot get away with it, you caused Chetan all this pain," an angry Avni raised her voice at the doctor.

"You must learn how to survive alone because the truth is– everyone leaves." The doctor showed no sign of atonement.

Chetan spoke softly, "You cannot undo what has been done. But you can stop more needless harm. Turn yourself in. Face justice."

The man nodded slowly, "I don't want to be Rishi. The years passed. I built a new life and an empire that no one can touch. Although I never stopped wondering about the child I had left behind, he was the reason I could build this huge empire. Now I cannot let the same child bring down this empire."

Both Avni and Chetan stayed numb. "I don't want to live as a monster. I have to admit the truth that apart from the three patients, the waiter, the gambler, and the alcoholic, I have never misbehaved or misled any of the patients. Very unfortunate that the reason for me to be dishonest with the profession also comes from the same unwanted child," the father sipped the coffee.

"How can you not heal from such vicious thoughts when you can heal hundreds of such people?" Avni spoke.

"The principles and skills we develop don't suit us. Healing is so hard when your inner child wants love, your teenage self wants revenge, and your current self only wants peace at any cost," the doctor choked for a moment.

Both Avni and Chetan understood that there was something unusual. "Don't worry, I have used the same poison that I used for your brother and mother," the doctor said as he pointed the duo's attention towards the coffee he drank.

"I had mixed poison in my coffee the moment you started revealing one death after the other. When you expect me to surrender, I don't have any other option apart from this." He finished the coffee in the mug.

Avni picked up her mobile to call an ambulance. Chetan stopped her.

"When the truth is offensive, we lie until we replace the lie with another lie. Every lie we tell incurs a debt to the truth, and that debt is paid sooner or later. He himself should pay." Chetan took the phone away from Avni while Adi took his last breath.

EPILOGUE

Avni and Chetan sat in front of the chair where Adi's body was.

"Now I understand why my mother never tried to treat my trauma when I was made fun of by my fellow mates in school for being a fatherless bastard. I could sense my mother's love throughout my childhood; however, I longed for my father figure to be present with me. The imagination I had whenever I thought about what would happen if my father were alive was pure fantasy, and I am thankful that I never knew about it when I was young." Chetan said.

"Parenthood doesn't mean giving birth to kids; it means taking up the responsibility to raise the kids. You cannot purchase it again once you have sold your responsibility. I am furious that I have been born to a greedy father and an irresponsible mother, but I am indebted to all the mothers like Indira who have made the name parenthood shine."

"It doesn't take a moment to let go of the things that burden us, but you should have the guts to hold on to them. I want to get hold of my mother, Indira, and be at her feet, cleaning with my tears for handling all the silent battles that she didn't speak of."

"My mother resisted her tears no matter the difficulty and always ensured I had a happy childhood. She never differentiated me from my brother Vinay; she raised us in the cradle of happiness. She has led me to say that she was with me, no matter how I handle a situation or what obstacle I face in achieving it. She forgave me for all my mistakes with a simple smile. Although it hurt like hell, she smiled like heaven. From now on, I will devote every moment to my mother with all love and sincerity."

"No one can have the guts and compassion my mother had, even if they take a thousand births. Vinay was the elderly one; my mom was all alone when her husband passed away. The adoption agency through which I was adopted is run by a charity funded by our family. She had responded humanely to the way I was given away."

"I was raised as an elder brother to hold the balance stronger. I feel sorry for my brother Vinay. Just my presence in their lives created this much havoc. Sometimes the strongest people are the ones who love beyond all faults, cry behind closed doors, and fight battles that nobody knows about. Giving birth may be difficult, but the pain it takes to nurture a kid into a responsible human cannot match it."

"My mother, Indira, had requested time for our marriage to sort this matter with Adi. She didn't even speak a word with me about the will, although she understood that my brother's death may be linked to the huge, unhealthy wealth that was scheduled to come into our lives."

"I never wanted to argue; I just wanted you to understand how I felt."

Now, Chetan spoke with Adi's body. "The mistake you made was not researching the solid facts."

"You have misunderstood or never understood the dignity of the culture my mother cultivated in us. If you had come up with the truth, we would have given you the entire wealth without thinking. My mother was just obligated to honor Nalini's deathbed wish." Chetan fumed at Adi's body.

Avni consoled Chetan and held that whatever he did was right, "I get it that you are tired, a tired where your soul says it needs rest as it is just tired of carrying around all the malignant stuff that you just dealt with. That kind of rest comes only with healing, which takes time. I am with you; you will be at peace soon."

"The peace looks good, but it's dangerous. Even though things seem fine initially, big problems are below the surface. My father was okay with giving up on me, but was never okay until he cost so many lives. All the victims have made peace with their problems: the alcoholic by killing Lalit, the gambler by killing my brother, and the waiter by killing both the gambler and the alcoholic. Everyone seems happy and content after making peace, but how long?"

"People act nice but are mad and don't trust each other. Peace is just pretended for a while. Secretly, people are making each other mad and hurt. Over time, the problems get bigger. Trust goes, and the hurt gets deeper. But on the outside, things still look okay. Only a few people can see that something is wrong."

"They pretend peace can't last forever. Eventually, it will break apart, and the anger will come out. People will start fighting and arguing."

"Right now, most people don't see the problems. The silence fools them. But the silence is fake. It hides the real feelings of anger and hate that will lead to big fights later on."

"The pretentious peace tricks people into thinking everything is okay. But it's making the problems worse the whole time. That's why it's so dangerous–it looks good on the outside but hides anger and problems that will explode eventually."

"The silence feels nice, but it won't last because it's built on lies and anger, not truth and kindness. That is the nature of the venomous peace–seeming harmony that harbors hatred, breeds betrayal, and sows the seeds of its own demise," Chetan finished.

❖

Weeks passed by. Chetan never disclosed the real culprit behind the murders. Everyone believed that the waiter had consumed poison to cope with the trauma.

As per the will, the entire property came under the name of Chetan. He married Avni and gave her the clinic to run under the same name without disturbing its purpose. He donated everything to a charity that treated people with emotional illness. He worked towards building a society where people made peace with kindness and truth. He continued his work by working towards providing justice to people as he had promised his mother.

ACKNOWLEDGEMENT

To my mother and sisters, whose unwavering support and encouragement continue to inspire me to strive for something better in life. Your love and belief in me are the greatest motivators I could ever ask for.

To all my audience – thank you for your support, encouragement, and for giving my words a space in your hearts.

The buzz and ongoing conversations surrounding my previous works, The Other Side of Silence and The Winless Battle, have fuelled my passion and motivated me to embark on this third journey. The excitement I feel while writing this book has already ignited my anticipation for my fourth, and I hope it continues to inspire and engage my readers as well.

I would like to express my deepest gratitude to the initial reviewers – Priyanka, Prathyusha, Soundarya, and Abhinav Kothapalli – for your valuable insights and encouragement.

A special thank you to Kavi from EBC, my first draft editor, for your guidance and keen eye that helped shape this work. Miss Milan, I am eternally grateful for your patience and willingness to lend me your ears – I must have rented them at least five times for feedback on my drafts!

Last but not least, I sincerely thank Shubham Singh and team Simplicité for believing in my work and giving it a platform. Achieving this milestone – having my book accepted for publication – is a significant accomplishment for me, and I am grateful for the opportunity to share my stories with the world.

ABOUT THE AUTHOR

Prashanth Chakkula is a software engineer and author of two works: The Other Side of Silence – The Hidden Strength and The Winless Battle. The Venomous Peace is his third book. He has a keen interest in traveling and follows sports closely. He can be reached at chakkulaprashanth@gmail.com.